THE CITY BELOW

A 2603 NOVEL

KORY M. SHRUM

This book is a work of fiction. Any references to historical events, real people, or real places have been used fictitiously. Other names, characters, places, and incidents are the product of the author's imagination. Any resemblance to actual persons, living or dead, business establishments, events, or locales is entirely coincidental.

No part of this book shall be reproduced or transmitted in any form or by any means without prior written permission of the publisher. Although every precaution has been taken in preparation of the book, the publisher and the author assume no responsibility for errors or omissions. Neither is any liability assumed for damages resulting from the use of information contained in this book or its misuse.

All rights reserved.

Copyright © 2020 by Kory M. Shrum
Cover design by Christian Bentulan
Edited by Sarah Kolb-Williams
Formatting by Alexandra Amor

ISBN: 978-1-949577-48-8

AN EXCLUSIVE OFFER FOR YOU

Connecting with readers is the best part of being a writer. I do that by sending 1–2 newsletters a month with subscribers-only ebooks, writing updates, first looks, behind-the-scenes content—and, of course, photos of my very cute dog.

If that sounds like something you'd enjoy, look for the special offer in the back of this book.

Thank you for reading!

Kory M. Shrum

ONE

GRACE BUTEO STOOD before the scanner in the Zone 2 precinct and allowed the machine to verify her biometrics. Arms out in a T, she drew a steady breath and rehearsed for the two hundredth time what she would say to Commander Adams upon seeing him.

The AI beeped, signaling completion of the scan. A light changed from red to green. The sealed door protecting the private sector of the precinct slid open, giving her access to the bio-sealed building.

The precinct bustled inside.

Officers, engaged in the enormity of their work for the zone, scurried like ants through the building. Grace might have reached the commander's office and their oh eight hundred appointment without fanfare if the scan itself had been the end of the verification process.

But as Grace crossed the threshold between the holding area and its guarded inner chambers, the AI spoke in a sweet, lilting voice. "Welcome back, Commander Buteo."

Footsteps faltered. Shuffling papers stilled. Conversations died.

Officer Lore Duchovny stood from his desk and began clapping so hard his dark hair fell forward into his face, half-hiding his set jaw and blazing eyes. But his clapping was soon swallowed by the cacophony of hundreds of hands, coming together over and over again—beating out a terrible rhythm that turned Grace's stomach to stone.

"Don't . . . please," she begged, feigning a gracious smile. It was hard to do when the right side of her face resisted, the scar tissue tight and unwilling to move.

The applause only worsened, giving way to words. Someone whistled.

"Thank you, Commander."

"My whole family thanks you, Commander."

"We are *so* glad you survived, Commander."

"It's *so* good to see your face again."

Grace doubted *that*. The burn scars eating away at her jaw and cheek weren't pretty to look at, and yet Lore Duchovny gazed at her as if he were looking into the face of an angel.

Hands reached for hers. Others touched her arm or squeezed her shoulder as she tried to push her way through the crowd. She was a saint, who, if touched in passing, would bless the believers.

They have a reason to believe in you, Gray.

Her dead husband's voice in her head was enough to wind her and turn her stone of a stomach cold.

Somehow, she continued down the line, passed from embrace to embrace, until it was Commander Adams himself before her at his open office door, his own smile bright.

His cheerful gaze faltered when it took in her right cheek, temple, and neck all shriveled above her collar. But he was quick to flick his eyes up to meet hers again.

He ushered her inside the office and closed the doors while the officers outside continued to clap and yip.

"Are you all right?" he asked. Commander Adams stood more than six feet tall, the black officer uniform tight across his broad shoulders. He was frowning at her. She wasn't sure what disturbed him—the new scars or her thinly veiled distress.

He seemed to take in her blind panic and the heat collecting in her face. She'd broken out in a sweat along the back of her neck, but hopefully he couldn't see that. She drew more breath and found her chest unwilling to expand.

"I wasn't expecting such a reception," she admitted and helped herself into the chair opposite his desk. That many people, that many bodies closing in on her—it had weakened her knees. Sitting down allowed her to affect some poise. "It . . . surprised me."

Adams put the desk between them by taking the opposite chair. "Every person in this precinct owes you their life. The least they can do is show a little gratitude."

"The card was enough."

He laughed, clearly surprised. "A card with a *thousand* signatures and endless praise will never be enough. Throw in a zonewide parade and a plaque, perhaps a statue in your honor, and *maybe* we'd be approaching proper compensation. But no, what you did was priceless."

"That's ridiculous," she said. A statue? Of *her*? It wasn't like she curbed an epidemic or removed all the radiation from the sky. "I hope you aren't serious."

"In fact, the funding is already approved."

She could only blink at him.

"Commander Buteo, you stopped the first mass-murder attempt in our zone in *centuries*. Those *terrorists* wanted to wipe out all of our officers in a single blow and would've succeeded if not for you. Hell, the IED was only six meters from Duchovny's wife and daughters and he damn well knows it."

There was something funny in the way Adams said the word *terrorists*. Not unlike *fairies* or *goblins*, as if this word were merely make-believe.

"But because of you, our officers are safe. Their families are safe. Our city is safe. And everyone knows what you paid for that safety."

What I paid.

The lives of her husband and her son. Her right arm from the elbow down. Half of her face.

It was the burned scar tissue that Commander Adams kept looking at now, as if that was the worst of it. How could she explain that her loss of beauty could never compare to all the happiness she buried in the Soul Grove?

"We're safe again, and we have you to thank for that. Let the city and its officers have their hero."

"I'm not a hero to Davion or Kaiden," she said.

"Your loss is . . . unfathomable," he agreed, tapping the surface of his desk. "But just because you couldn't save two lives, that doesn't change the fact that you *did* save thousands upon *thousands*. The officers' and their families', to be sure, but also the lives of our city's citizens. What would have happened to them if our borders had fallen?"

She barely heard this. She thought, *they weren't just any lives. They were the only two lives that mattered.*

"Still, I'm getting complaints from the mayor that this event seems to have stalled immigration requests. Hopefully, if we have a couple of quiet months ahead of us, the number of applicants will go back up and he'll get off our backs."

Grace understood that the lack of crime was one of Zone 2's most attractive features. But all the centermost zones—Zones 1 through 6—could make such a boast. Violent crime prevailed only in the outermost districts.

Despite the mayor's concerns that their crime ratings might rise by a mere one percent or even two percent, Grace knew that people would sell everything they owned to have a place here.

Her husband Davion had always told her to be grateful for her job. To be grateful that petty, nonviolent crimes made up the bulk of her work. That her livelihood required creative problem-solving solutions rather than the strong arm of the law. The only real danger to their zone was cybercrime: hacking, thefts, or fraud—and she was trained for all of it.

It's not like the outer zones, Gray, he'd told her. *Where someone will slit your kid's throat for your last gallon of water.*

Yes, she knew what Davion would say about all of this if he'd lived.

That she was lucky. That there were others who would give up their husbands, their children, their face, and *both* arms just to be able to walk down their streets free.

She understood this, but she didn't care.

She wanted her family back.

"So what do you think? About the statue? I believe they're considering bronze." Adams waited for her reaction, clearly expecting some outpouring of gratitude or delight.

She'd used most of her energy to pull herself from bed, bathe, and arrive at the precinct on time. What little fight she had left was lost to the mob outside. She couldn't spare any energy for a diplomatic response.

"I think it's stupid," she said. "If it can't be stopped, I can only hope you'll put it somewhere I'll never see it."

"It would be less for you than for the people of this city," he said, his excitement deflating. "The attack frightened them. They need a visual reminder that they're safe here. That their zone has a guardian."

He flicked his eyes down, activating his corneal display. His eyes glowed blue. "I've just received the notice from the hospital saying you can return to work."

"I'm fit for duty," she assured him.

He flicked his glowing blue eyes up to meet hers. "Do you really feel ninety days is long enough to recover from your personal losses?"

Grace used her considerable will to remain calm. "Are you referring to the prosthetic arm, the burned face, or the dead family, Adams?"

Adams sputtered.

He'd better accept the hospital's assessment, because the only thing worse than being applauded for an act of heroism she deeply regretted would be going home without the job she'd sacrificed all her happiness for.

"All I have left is this job, and I plan to do it. Lucky for me you have no authority to decide whether or not I'm fit to be here." Her voice was cold.

And she spoke truth. He was voted into his post the same as she was. He was her *co*-commander, with no more power than she had. If he wanted her removed, he'd have a hell of time achieving it.

He bristled and sat up straighter in his seat. "Honestly, it's great to have you back. This precinct needs both of its commanders, especially after last night."

Her heart kicked in her chest. "What happened last night?"

"Not an explosive device," he was quick to add. "Just a theft. Viscosity Inc. had over two dozen organs stolen from their South Hanscomb facility. The case came in at oh two hundred."

"A public or private building?"

"Private and fully bio-sealed," he confirmed, leaning his forearms on his desk. His eyes lit with that slight, reflective blue light as his gaze reviewed the details invisible to her. "Only those with clearance can enter and exit the facility."

"How many had access during the time of theft?"

"About sixty employees to the organ chambers. Over two hundred were coded for the lab itself. The whole company employs more than twenty thousand people. It's enormous."

"And the biometric system detected nothing?"

"There's a lot of data to sift through. It will be a time-consuming case."

"Time is all I have now." She shouldn't have said this. Such comments would initiate conversations she didn't want to have.

"Grace . . ." he began and then seemed to think better of it. "When I mentioned that you'd returned from leave, the CEO, Getty Peters, was thrilled and requested you for the investigative assessment. I'll try not to take it personally."

When a crime was confirmed in the city, it was the commander's job to complete the initial assessment and determine if the security of the zone had been compromised. That was her utmost responsibility—to keep the zone safe and secured from all threats, inside and out.

Once the assessment was complete, the investigation was dissected and tasks were delegated to the precinct's inspectors. A commander, after all, was part team leader, part politician. Particularly diplomatic when interzone action with other commanders was needed or tending to the delicate nerves of city officials was required.

She supposed this would be the first of many requests,

and she would be the favorite for a while. And why should it matter if she buried herself in work?

Who waited for her at home? No one.

"Once you solve this," Adams said, lacing his fingers together, "I think the zone will relax. The network breach and explosion frightened the community. With Commander Buteo out in the streets again, asking questions . . . well, it will cheer them up to see you. The moment your name sounds in the Informed Citizen Bulletin—" His voice dropped to a comic imitation of a newscaster. "'*Commander Buteo saves the day again*'—it will quell the unrest that has built while you were…away."

While she lay in a hospital bed healing third-degree burns and having her arm replaced, he meant.

"I'll get started then."

Adams smiled. "I'll tell them to expect you. While you're out, I'll finish up my ninety-day cache. I'll have it to you by the end of the day so you can be brought up to speed on all that's happened in your absence. Unless you want me to join you for a verbal debriefing?"

"I don't mind working solo," she said. In fact, it might be a blessed reprieve to abandon herself to the job without forcing smiles or combatting kind words. She needed a break from the endless thoughts that circled her mind like buzzards.

"Oh, you won't be alone," Adams said.

She frowned. Her face resisted it. "I won't?"

"Your request for an assistant inspector was approved while you were in the hospital. I oversaw the onboarding myself. Inspector Heron Jane is at your disposal. He's . . . different."

Grace rose from her seat, declaring the return interview over. "I look forward to meeting him."

"Wait, Grace." Adams twisted his hands together.

She paused in the doorway and turned back to face him. The gentleness on Adams's face made her skin crawl.

He was looking at her scars again. "I know it will be hard to put what's happened behind you, but you have to try."

She gestured at the office around her. "What do you think I'm trying to do here?"

"Just try not to torture yourself."

She grasped the door handle and laughed. It was a bitter, sharp sound. "Do you know me at all, Adams?"

"I do," he said, his expression part concern, part fear. "And I've never known you to let sleeping dogs lie."

TWO

GRACE CROSSED the pedestrian walk to the auto stop opposite the precinct. She could have ordered second-level transport and coasted above ground-level traffic as her authority afforded. But a slower commute would give her a chance to compose herself. She'd underestimated how hard it would be to look everyone in the eye and pretend she was okay when she wasn't.

It hadn't been the sly glances at her scarred face or their soft, apologetic eyes, both of which she'd prepared herself for. It hadn't even been the meaningless small talk, which she found exhausting on the best of days.

It had been the admiration she'd found unbearable. Their love dripped with pity.

Her PNS pinged. "Your auto will arrive in ninety-three seconds, Commander Buteo."

Have the autos ever run anybody over? Kaiden had asked, his thick curling hair outrageous on the top of his head as he'd blinked gorgeous brown eyes up at her. Specks of sunlight sparked in them. He had her eyes.

They have sensors on all sides, she'd told him. *They'll stop before they hit you.*

They go so fast.

They do, but they're also very good at stopping.

Kaiden. Her chest compressed so suddenly that she reached out and seized the safety rail framing the arrival platform. The pavement danced beneath her and no matter which of the embedded plastic particulates she focused on, she couldn't undo the knot in her chest.

The auto rolled up to the curb and the door lifted like a swan unfurling its wing to usher her inside.

"Welcome, Commander Buteo. Please watch your—"

Grace all but threw herself into the dark interior of the auto and the door sealed itself behind her.

"We are pleased you've chosen CityRide for your transportation needs today, Commander Buteo," the AI chimed. "My name is Charity and I will be your driver today. Can I confirm that your destination is Viscosity Incorporated? Three thirty-three Halogen Boulevard?"

"Yes."

There was a pause as the AI computed the address. "That is an eleven-minute ride by level one transport. The rate for this transaction is $24. Confirm order?"

"Yes."

A *ping* resonated through the auto's interior. "Your account has been deducted $24 for this transaction. Thank you for choosing CityRide. Safe. Fast. CityRide. We value your business."

The automatic safety harness fastening across her chest didn't make her breathing any easier. She desperately tried to suck in more air and think of anything but Kaiden.

Kaiden with his soft, wild hair.

Kaiden with his goofy, crooked grin, one of the front teeth only halfway out of its upper gum.

"You do not have any music stored on your channels, Commander Buteo. Would you like me to play something for you? I have 'News' or 'Music.' I also have a large selection of ambient noise such as 'Thunderstorms' and . . ."

Kaiden with his smart questions that sometimes stunned her into laughing.

Kaiden with his penchant for building and playing piano and his endless requests for a dog—a real one, not a robotic one.

And they were two months from caving and buying it, despite the horrendous fees and taxes.

Kaiden . . .

"No."

"No music selected. Please let me know if you need any temperature or light adjustments within the cabin—"

"Nothing, dammit! I don't need anything!" Her voice echoed so loudly in the enclosed space her ears rang. Her heart thrummed hard against her ribs. She could feel the pulse building in her temple, pressure rising.

The AI governing the auto seemed offended by her outburst, responding with cold silence. It was only a voice bot, rattling off a preprogrammed selection of choices for customers. Most likely it was searching for a response that matched her words. And yet, illogically, Grace felt bad for yelling at it.

It occurred to her, not for the first time, that perhaps she was losing her mind. And why not? Hadn't people broken down for less than the loss of their entire family? Why should she be any different?

Because you're strong. The most willful and stubborn person I've ever met, Davion's voice replied in her head.

Blessedly, the cabin dimmed and Grace was left in silence with her throbbing temples. She covered her face with her hands.

She tried to focus on anything, anything but Kaiden's face framed in the passenger's side window of her auto, mouthing *Mom* the second before it exploded.

Four wheels were blown off into the balmy night and the whole vehicle lifted six meters off the ground, underbelly in flames.

The blue light of her network responder caught the corner of her eye. "Your heart rate and blood pressure are elevated. Run the CALM program?"

She pinched the bridge of her nose. "Yes."

"When you find your emotions suffocating," the prerecorded therapist said, "bring your attention to the present moment. To the sensations in your body, and if that is too much, to the area around you. What do you see? What do you smell? Do you feel the energy in your hands?"

Her hands were trembling.

Her throat was so tight that her mouth remained open in a silent, strangled cry.

"Focus on this moment. What do you see, Grace?"

Her eyes darted around the interior of the cabin but could see nothing except light reflected through her tears. She blinked, and the auto came into sharp relief.

"Describe what you see. Aloud. Where are you?"

"I'm in a CityRide auto."

"Excellent, Grace. Please continue."

"I see the freeway. All the autos. The buildings flying past. I'm sure if this auto ran into a building at full speed, that'd be the end of me."

"You are safe now, Grace," it prompted.

She hesitated, her eyes sliding over the vehicles moving in the same direction she was. A sea of white beetles scurrying down the rose-gold boulevards.

"What else do you see?"

"I don't know."

"You're doing great, Grace. Tell me more."

"Uh, mostly there's plants. Flowers. CO_2 neutralizers."

The pounding in her head lessened. She was able to exhale fully now. Exhaustion pressed in. She'd only been working for an hour and she was already *so* tired. That didn't bode well.

"Describe something you like about this moment."

"I like . . . the electric whine." The sound made it impossible for her to think.

"That sounds lovely. Please describe it for me. I'm not sure I've ever heard it."

"Of course you've never heard it. You're a robot."

The program was meant to continue prompting her until her heart rate returned to acceptable levels. Therefore, it was impervious to her insults.

She sighed. "The autos have this thin whine as they roll. I don't know if it's made by the tires themselves or if it's the sound of energy going into the auto's battery."

"I'm not sure I understand."

"The tires spinning against the road creates kinetic energy. It charges the auto, and any leftover power is sent to the zone's power grid. Kaiden did a report on it."

Kaiden. Again, that crooked grin and his small hand slipping into hers. So warm.

Fresh tears pricked her eyes.

"That sounds lovely, Grace. I see why you enjoy it."

A second-level emergency transport sailed over her, its titanium legs momentarily dimming the interior of her cabin as it passed at three times the speed of the level one transport.

She recognized the red fire department stripe on the carrier's exterior.

"There's a fire responder passing overhead."

"Pick something closer to you. Focus now. Does something beautiful catch your eye?"

Grace understood that beautiful or curious things were meant to calm the mind, but as she surveyed the buildings of downtown, she only felt assaulted by the greenery. And not just by the rooftop gardens or flower boxes crowding every window. Every pillar, roadside railing, and sidewalk were covered with endless tendrils.

It was a jungle, hot and humid, pressing in on her. Like a cloth over her mouth and nose.

"Pick something else to focus on, Grace."

But the only objects not covered in plant life were the golden solar panels serving as every building's exterior. They regarded her impassively like large insect eyes.

"Is there anything you can appreciate?"

"A day has only so many hours," she said, and exhaled. "I appreciate that."

At last, the knot in her chest loosened. She no longer had to hold the belt away from her as if it were suffocating her.

"Your heart rate is within acceptable parameters now. You did great. I'm proud of you, Grace. Before the program is terminated, I would like you to say something with me."

Grace detested this part of the MindCare program. But the snub-nosed therapist at the hospital had insisted that this software be installed into her lenscape before she returned to work. It had been her only stipulation, and Grace had seen no way to refuse her.

"Please repeat after me: I am grateful for this moment."

Grace rolled her eyes. "I am grateful for this moment."

"Perfect. Repeat this as often as you need. Take care of

yourself, Grace. Remember, you are loved. You are needed. You are important to us."

Grace threw herself against the auto's seat and covered her face with her hands.

Loved. Needed. Important.

And the reason why her family was dead.

THREE

"WE WILL ARRIVE at your destination in two minutes, Commander Buteo. The temperature outside our cabin is thirty-five degrees Celsius today. Sunny. Today's air particulate rating is forty-eight. Acceptable. Today's UV rating is moderate. Protection is highly suggested. Our records indicate that you have not yet listened to today's Informed Citizen report. Would you like to play it now?"

"No, thank you." Grace recognized the large, luminous building up ahead with its flashing sign.

"Announcement delayed for four hours."

The auto pulled up to the auto stop adjacent to Viscosity Inc. and its door lifted, revealing a woman and three children waiting to climb in after her.

"Enjoy your day, Commander Buteo. And we thank you again for your patronage."

She excused herself, maneuvering around the cluster onto the covered walk. Her eyes kept straying to the ostentatious sign on the front of the Viscosity skyscraper.

Slowly, her ears detected the ripple rolling through the crowd.

"Commander Buteo."

"Oh Springer, that's her."

"Her *poor face*—"

"And her son was only—"

Someone called after her. Fortunately, unlike in the police precinct, it was easy to hide herself in the crowd.

Whoever wanted to speak with her was swept away by the tide of bodies.

When the pedestrian sign illuminated and the AI commanded *WALK*, she crossed the wide boulevard toward the building's large paneled door.

Viscosity. Securing your future.

"Please stand on the sensor and be as still as possible," the AI instructed. The small videogram by the front door blinked and flashed in unison with the voice.

The exterior door slid open.

"Verified. Welcome to Viscosity, Commander Buteo. Please enter reception for complete scanning."

This was a tedious part of her job. Most city employees had only to deal with the biometric scan of one or two secured buildings in the course of their day. But the precinct and nearly every other building that she visited in her line of work was secured and bio-sealed to one degree or another. She felt like half of her job was simply presenting herself to the network for confirmation.

But they have good reason to be cautious, don't they? she thought. At present, the precinct was only half secured, the other half open to the public so that officers remained accessible to the constituents they served.

That might change now after the attack.

The unsecured portion of the precinct building was where the first of two IEDs had been hidden: in a storage closet near the center of the precinct, just seven meters from her own office. Had she missed that explosive as well as the second . . .

She pushed down the thoughts before the MindCare program could activate itself again. If she had to spend another second describing the beauty of flowers today, she would lose it.

She assumed the scan position, hands loose at her side, palms open, and legs spread, while the scanner recorded her biometrics and compared them against those stored in the network.

Her ear shape, the veins in her palms, iris and retina recognition, facial recognition. She wondered if the new arm, the replacement they'd created for her in the hospital, would pass this test. The hospital assured her they'd updated her new biometrics in the network, zonewide, to include the new arm. She'd passed the inspection at the precinct, but this felt different.

"Please state your name."

"Commander Grace Buteo." She hated declaring herself. It was ridiculous. But all network signatures included full titles, and saying something as simple as "Grace Buteo" might trigger the alarm and delay her entry.

The light changed from red to green. "Welcome to Viscosity Inc., Commander. Please check in at the front desk in section A2."

Her lenscape automatically linked with the building's private server. The network overlaid her reality with a guiding arrow, blinking, showing her where to find the A2 desk as she crossed from the foyer into the receiving area.

Once the reception desk came into view, the arrow transformed into a green checkmark beside a pretty receptionist's face and disappeared, leaving her field of vision unhindered again.

Without the checkmark, she was able to see the tall man standing at the desk for the first time. He leaned against it, flashing perfect, obviously altered teeth at the woman behind the counter. She laughed riotously, throwing her head back.

Grace stepped up to the counter. "Hello."

The pretty receptionist blushed crimson as she met Grace's eyes. "Welcome, Commander Buteo. Thank you so much for coming. We've been anxiously awaiting your arrival."

I can tell.

The man's demeanor changed. The relaxed, roguish posture he'd adopted for the receptionist stiffened. The devilish smile took on a formal grimness, and before Grace understood what was happening, he was brushing his hand against the back of hers.

Her reader accepted his profile share, which provided his name, zone of origin, and current business in the zone.

"Commander Buteo, I'm Inspector Jane. Heron Jane."

"My assistant?" she said, pushing the profile aside.

He flinched at the words. "Yes."

"I didn't mean it as an insult, Inspector," she said. She hoped the appropriate honorific helped.

"I'm not insulted," he said, the stiffness only worsening as he withdrew his hand. "I *am* here to assist you."

The pretty receptionist looked down and away as her earpiece lit blue. Then she met Grace's gaze with a fresh smile. "They're waiting for you in the east laboratory. If you would be so kind as to accept our welcome cache, a map will automatically be downloaded to your lenscape."

"Thank you."

"Can I do anything else for you?" the receptionist asked. She finally let her smile glide toward Heron hopefully.

"No, thank you," he said. The formality with which he now regarded her made her pretty eyes flutter, the disappointment obvious.

Grace turned away. She completed the network onboarding and received Viscosity's welcome cache.

"Map," she said. An overview of her position on the ground level appeared in her lenscape, laid seamlessly over her reality.

"East laboratory," she requested, and another dutiful green arrow guided her toward the elevators located at the center of the building.

Inspector Jane caught up to her at the elevator doors, stepping in after her.

You wanted this, she reminded herself. To be out in the world, yes. To give her restless mind something to do, absolutely. She'd wanted pure distraction. The *peopling* part was the price she had to pay for it.

"Heron Jane is an unusual name," she said as the doors closed. She tried to ease her shoulders away from her ears. "Yet I feel like I've heard it somewhere."

"My mother was a famous ornithologist," he said simply, his hands in the loose pockets of his pants.

Jane.

She turned and scrutinized him. "Dr. Victoria Jane?"

He smiled, looking almost amused. "That's the one."

"Why didn't you pursue science?" she asked. "With your mother, I suspect that no door would've been closed to you."

"And spend the rest of my life trying to live up to her?" He laughed as if this was an old joke he'd grown tired of telling. "I could never do her justice."

"I'm sure she doesn't see it that way." Naturally, Grace's traitorous mind slid toward her own son.

I want to be a commander like you, Mommy. I want to keep the city safe too.

She leaned her weight heavily on the elevator's wall.

"Are you all right?" Jane asked. He'd reached out to her and froze, realizing what he was doing midmotion. Slowly, he withdrew his hand.

"It's just the . . ." She searched for the word that wouldn't come.

"Acceleration? Velocity? Ascension?" he offered.

She shook her head, desperately wishing he would step back more and give her some air.

"It's just the elevator," she finished weakly.

His posture relaxed. "Yes, I find them offensive myself. It's one of the least evolved inventions to exist today. The modern elevator has been in use for over *seven hundred years* and yet it's had few improvements. Talk about resting on your laurels."

She wasn't sure what to say to this, so she said nothing. Obviously he was trying to cheer her up, but he seemed nervous. She saw it in the way he kept coming up onto the balls of his feet.

Was she making him nervous? Likely. She was the boss, and it was his first day.

When she heard his sharp intake of breath, she intervened. "Why Heron?"

He froze. In fact, he looked terrified, his wide eyes shining.

His reaction didn't match her question, so she clarified the best she could. "Why did she name you *Heron*? Of all the birds?"

"Oh," he said. Whatever he'd thought she meant by *why* was obviously worse than mild curiosity regarding the origin of a name. "When the sea levels first rose, before we started to move inland and rebuild, a lot of the animals died—mammals, birds, fish—either through habitat loss, pollution, or starvation. But one of the birds that did best, despite the terrible conditions, was the heron. Do you know what herons look like?"

Grace admitted that she did not.

"They've got a spear-like beak and very long legs, both of which are pretty useful when fishing in high waters. They're waders, which means they can walk out into deeper water in order to find their prey. They don't mind heat, and they can migrate. And they do as well in the wild as in more cosmopolitan environments. They're very resourceful birds that can survive just about anywhere."

"Your mother has faith in your abilities."

He laughed. "My mother is an optimist, yes."

Grace surveyed him with the corner of her eye. An expensive suit. A clean, handsome face. When he reached up to scratch his nose, she noted the individual signal booster ring fitted to his right hand. Something like that must have cost twice Grace's salary. She suspected that like his avian namesake, he was surviving all right.

"I don't mind the name," he said. "It was better than the alternative."

"What was the alternative?"

"If I'd been female, she was going to name me Egret," he said with a grin. And, realizing she didn't get the joke, added, "It's another wader. Snow-white feathers."

It occurred to her he might be evaluating her, measuring her as ruthlessly as she was him. Her profile must have been useless for this task. When he'd brushed her hand, he would have learned only *Grace Helena Buteo, Commander, Zone 2.*

Some profiles were ostentatiously detailed. Favorite music, favorite food, favorite stores, education history, marital status or partner affiliation, family or friend connections, gender expressions, languages spoken, political stances, group affiliations, and so on.

For Heron, anything he wanted to know about his commander, he would have to ask.

And what *did* he think of her?

Her stiff form. Her borderline inability to smile. The scars along her right temple and cheek. He must see the scars. It was her diminished right side that faced him.

"What about your name?" he asked. "Did your mother want you to be a dancer or something?"

"Grace was her grandmother's name," she said.

The elevator opened, and they were greeted by a scientist marching toward them. A small, dark woman with onyx eyes and open arms. For a terrifying moment, Grace thought she was going to be embraced, but instead, the scientist punctuated the exaggerated gesture by clapping her hands together.

"Welcome, welcome. I'm Dr. Loba Cyrah, I would like to thank you for your service—"

Please don't.

"—Commander Buteo. I'm so sorry for your loss."

The perfunctory "Thank you" was managed despite her tightening throat. Heron offered to brush hands with Dr. Cyrah, but Grace saw the scientist hesitate.

Only reluctantly did she finally offer her profile. Grace politely refused. There were many ways to access public profiles, and she'd reached her limit of physical contact for the day.

"This way, if you please." Dr. Cyrah waved them toward the large glass chamber of the lab.

Grace caught Heron watching her with a strange expression she couldn't quite place.

"After you," he said and gestured toward Dr. Cyrah.

"It's my understanding that two dozen organs were stolen?" Grace began.

The door opened for the scientist after she paused long enough to have her body scanned for clearance. She held the door so that Grace and Heron could follow her before the chamber sealed itself.

"Twenty-six to be exact. Well, twenty-seven if you count each eye individually," she said. "Eight kidneys, six livers, four hearts, three pancreases, three lungs, a thymus, and even a pair of eyes. What a monster they wish to make!"

Grace smiled politely at the joke. "And you're certain the lab is bio-sealed."

"Yes. Our system has never failed us. Because the organs are so fragile, you see, a reliable system is paramount to our success. Without it, we'd be out of business in a month. See for yourself."

The doctor led them down a long aisle with metal tables positioned on either side. Each rectangular slab was divided into eight equal-sized squares, and in the square quadrants lay clear sacks with colorless organs inside.

The tubes and fluids gave the organs a buoyancy. But to Grace, they looked like strange sea creatures. All jelly sacks and tentacles.

She suspected Heron knew what animal she was thinking of but didn't want to ask him. No doubt his own mother would have had him learn every animal. And more about plants, light, wind, and water than she herself would ever know.

All the things I'll never teach Kaiden.

Grace coughed to clear her constricting throat.

Dr. Cyrah rested her hand on the shining table, and its color changed. The entire surface was a sensor, Grace realized, monitoring the organs' condition and progress through their sack-like membranes.

Dr. Cyrah licked her lips and said, "Fifty-eight employees watch these organs in lab fourteen day and night. Even when there are no human eyes on them, a hundred computers relentlessly record every temperature shift, drop in salinity, tissue deterioration, and so forth. *Anything* that could possibly change in these little environments is automatically corrected or reported to ensure that the organs are not compromised."

"Yes," Heron said, nodding. "Imagine what would happen if an organ was unavailable because of some lab malfunction. Angry customers don't make for good business!"

Dr. Cyrah glared at him.

Grace had seen the commercials while she recuperated in the hospital. They were horrible, actually. Viscosity seemed to revel in the weakness of the human body, reminding viewers that limbs, organs, or even eyes could be torn from their sockets at any time and *what will you do if Viscosity isn't there for you?*

Choose Viscosity. Secure your future.

"Fortunately, the organs taken were from storage. There are no active requests for any that were lost. Assuming our consumers remain healthy for the next sixty days, we remain confident that we can replace the organs before they are needed. We can replace and grow any biological tissue here. Your skin, for example."

Grace looked up and met the scientist's dancing eyes. The woman reached out and traced the air above Grace's right cheek, first up to her temple and then down her throat, continuing until she reached Grace's navel. She was implying that burn covered her chest, her breast, and part of her stomach on that side.

It did. But how could she possibly know that?

"Plasticity did your arm, didn't they?" Dr. Cyrah asked. She clicked her tongue as if she despised the name of the rival company.

"Yes." She glanced down at the smooth, bare skin and realized it must be obvious that her arm was bionic. It was a perfect mirror replica of her left, but with all the scarring on this side of her body, no way her arm would be so unblemished.

"The scarring on your face and neck looks to be third-degree burns, some fourth, am I right? We could regrow all of that and graft it right on. Several treatments under the Selsie light, and we could have you perfect again in eight or nine sessions."

Perfect. Nothing in her life would ever be perfect again.

"I elected not to treat the scars," Grace said with a pointed stare.

Grace hadn't wanted her wound erased. If she had to remember what happened every day of her life, why not the rest of the world? Besides, cosmetic work could only be done legally with the permission of the recipient.

The scientist squirmed. "If it's a matter of price, we can give you a steep discount. It would be excellent publicity for us, and we could even make you—"

Grace's blood pressure was rising again. She felt the heat in her face.

"Is it true you grow headless specimens here?" Heron asked. He drummed his fingers on the tabletop, drawing the doctor's eyes to him.

Dr. Cyrah looked rightfully offended by the question, her little stub of a nose turning up. "That was before my time. Besides, they *had* to be headless. People were concerned about the implication of full-bodied clones, even if they were kept in a coma state. It was considered unethical. So the heads and bodies were grown separately."

"I don't see how that's possible given the way the neck, throat, and spinal column connect and—"

"They didn't have—" Dr. Cyrah's mouth snapped shut. She looked ready to burst.

"Is anyone missing?" Grace asked, glad Heron had done a wonderful job of turning the conversation away from her scars. Grace gestured around the lab before pointing down the row of long tables, toward the other workers inspecting the equipment and sealed organs.

"Only one," Dr. Cyrah said, tugging at the bottom of her lab coat, her cheeks still tinted pink. "We have a technician, Ravee Kapur, who didn't show up for his oh nine hundred shift this morning."

"Can we get his address and contact information?" Grace asked. She suspected that if the criminal was intelligent—and one must be to exit a bio-sealed building with twenty-six organs discreetly in tow—it would be best to show up for work the next day and answer all the questions as if nothing had happened.

For this reason, Grace expected to encounter their thief during the interviews, not hiding from the authorities. Of course, people did surprise her from time to time with their stupidity. For example, take the bomber who went after the precinct. Lix Richards had remained too close to the scene, not hiding himself at all.

"We'd like a list of all persons permitted in this area," Heron said, rather haughtily.

"Of course."

Something caught Grace's eye. She moved toward the back of the lab, wandering past the glittering, clean tables and softly whirring tech equipment. She excused herself as she squeezed past busy workers and their blinking monitoring systems. Something kept clicking.

Click *clack*. Click *clack*.

On the wall was a large portrait of all the workers. Grace was able to spot Dr. Loba Cyrah on the far right, her smile bright, her shoulders pulled back in a picture-perfect pose.

She picked out a few of the other faces: two men and three women who were working the machines closest to her now. But most of the faces were strangers.

Dr. Cyrah stopped beside her. "This was taken at the instructional seminar two Octobers ago."

"Ah, yes," Heron said, coming around the tables to squint up at it. "This is Dr. Hillinger's method."

"What is?" Dr. Cyrah asked. Her irritation hadn't left her voice completely. As smitten as the first-floor receptionist had been with the young inspector, it seemed Heron's charms did not extend to Dr. Cyrah.

Strangely, that made Grace like Heron a little more.

"Dr. Hillinger is a psychologist who proposed that a feeling of home could be created simply by seeing yourself in that place. It mimics a sense of belonging created in home environments, the primary place we see such photographs. Hillinger was the one who encouraged employee photos in workplaces to promote loyalty. Of course, this one is rather impersonal. Close-up and individual shots would be better. Especially photos with the employees doing something they love. Everyone in this photo looks hungry."

"That's ridiculous," Dr. Cyrah said. "Science says it's memories that create affection for a place."

"Dr. Hillinger wouldn't disagree. Warm memories of a place do create affection, as does familiarity, but more important is *seeing* yourself."

Grace saw that Dr. Cyrah was on the verge of exploding into a counterargument.

"Are these all the people who have access to this lab?" she asked. Grace scanned the portrait, guessing how many faces she saw.

"Actually, yes," Dr. Cyrah said.

"And the man you mentioned? The missing technician?"

"Here is Ravee." Dr. Cyrah pointed to a tall man with thick black hair, eyes that were just a tad too close to one another, and a nose that stuck out rather long on his face. He was positioned at Dr. Cyrah's right arm.

Grace opened her camera software and snapped three photos of the portrait.

"I hate to say it—" Dr. Cyrah began.

But you will anyway, Grace thought.

"—but it *has* to be Ravee who stole the organs. He is the only one who could have overridden the doors and removed the organs from the sensors without tripping the alarms we have in place."

"He isn't the only one," Heron countered. "He's just the only *missing* one."

Grace wondered where Adams had found this man. His investigation methods were not at all standard. Where was he trained?

It was important to remain calm and assured in initial interviews. Absolutely no conflict of any kind was to be introduced. All behavior should encourage the flow of information, uninterrupted. Even if it was only lies pouring from someone's mouth, it was still data that could be sifted and used, either for or against the evidence that would come later. Hindering data at this phase of the investigation severely limited their options. And conflict *always* hindered.

So why in the world was Heron baiting Dr. Cyrah?

Grace needed to resume control of the interview. "Was Ravee familiar with the alarms used to monitor the condition of the organs?"

"Yes, and he knew that the slightest error would immediately trigger the alarm."

"He must've expected an immediate response," she continued.

"Oh yes. We are very prompt. Even minutes of incorrect incubation can cause tissue death," Dr. Cyrah said. "Whoever took the organs had to know how to harvest them from the monitoring system and disable the alarms. Ravee serviced the computers himself. He could have done it easily."

"What about the other lab workers?" Heron asked. "Wouldn't someone have seen him taking *two dozen* organs?"

The top of Dr. Cyrah's ears glowed red. "We think it happened during the shift change. There's a five-minute window between second and third shift when the lab is empty. Ravee is usually the first one here."

"And when does that changeover happen?" Grace asked.

"Just before midnight."

He looked ready to speak again but Grace shot him a look. Heron fell silent at once.

"Thank you," Grace said, to both Dr. Cyrah and Heron. "That's all we need for now. We have more than enough to begin. We'll be in touch."

She gave the portrait one last lingering look.

FOUR

ON THE SUNNY street outside Viscosity, Grace took a deep breath.

Heron stepped up beside her and did the same. "Yes, there's something suffocating about laboratories. They're completely unnatural. My mother says science must be done out here."

He gestured at the wide boulevard divided by the second-level transport above and the whizzing white City-Rides below. A second-level transport, looking like a large silver disk, flew by in the direction of the hospital.

"She had no right to imply that you needed a new face. That was incredibly unprofessional. And incorrect. Your face is lovely."

"She only wanted publicity for Viscosity."

He seemed to consider this. "It was still horribly rude."

His anger surprised her. They'd just met. There was no reason for him to feel defensive on her behalf.

Grace squinted up at him on the sidewalk. "Where did you do your training?"

"De la Hoya Academy."

"Is Commander Huang still there in the barn?" This was a deliberate test because there was no Commander Huang, nor was there a barn—at least none that she'd seen in her four years inside what the recruits called the Castle, a ruthless training facility in Zone 23.

"Didn't see a barn and never met a Commander Huang," Heron said simply. "Loved Commander Zhou though. And Commanders Cross and Ramirez. Ramirez still has that tiny dog."

"The Peekatease?" Grace asked, recognizing all the names he'd just regurgitated to her.

"It must be a hundred years old," he exaggerated with a warm smile. "And blind in both eyes."

It had been blind in *one* eye when Grace had been at the Castle years ago. She was older than Heron. In fact, he was closer to Davion's age than her own.

If he had done his training properly and at one of the best facilities in the country, then why did he unsettle her?

Her thoughts were interrupted by his beeping ring. He turned it over to review the scrolling inscription. This wasn't the booster ring meant to amplify his PNS's power. This one was made of a slightly darker metal. Grace tried to read the small inscription rolling along this glossy surface, but the glare from the sun made it impossible.

"The UV rating has gone up. Do you have a SunGuard?" he asked.

He meant the subcutaneous implant that had just hit the markets last summer. For a steep price, one could have automatic whole-body protection against excessive UV light and radiation.

Heron must've thought her far wealthier than she was. She could never indulge in the body mods that the younger generations seemed to favor now. Not without serious rebudgeting.

"No." She pulled a pen from her pocket. She pointed the pen toward the ground, and it expanded, first doubling, then tripling in length. At last, a circle disc unfolded to its full size, revealing the sunbrella.

From beneath its shade, Grace saw that many people walked around unguarded. How much faster was the ring on Heron's finger at detecting atmospheric shifts? Or was he wrong?

They'd managed half a block toward the nearest auto stop when she heard the familiar *chirp, chirp, chirp* of an Informed Citizen bulletin.

Everyone around her paused on the street at the same moment, preparing to have their lenscapes overrun by the zone's network.

Dearest Citizens, please note that the UV rating for Zone 2 has risen from Orange-Elevated to Red-Risk. Please seek protection immediately. If you are seen without protection in any public area, you will be ticketed. Remember: Information is Liberation.

The bulletin dropped away until Grace saw only the sidewalk and the shine of her black shoes. The others around her resumed motion.

"Are you usually the first to know something?" Grace murmured, more to herself than to the inspector beside her.

"I should think that's a wonderful asset for you," he said with a tight-lipped smile. "Considering that I'm at your disposal."

She caught the tone of *disposal*.

"That's twice that you've seemed offended at the idea of being my assistant. This isn't servitude, Inspector. If you don't want the position—"

"No," he said, too quickly. He pinched his eyes shut. "I want it. You'll have to forgive my sense of humor, Commander."

Grace didn't believe for a moment that this was simply misunderstood humor. But she also didn't have it in her to address compatibility issues today. She had been the one to ask for an assistant, and no matter who she'd received, she would have had to train them. He was as good as any. An assistant inspector was a perfect match for the smaller tasks she found tedious and exhausting.

I'll figure the rest out later, she thought.

"How would you like to proceed with the investigation, Commander? Any idea where we might find twenty-six organs?" Heron's reserve had returned.

She didn't like his stiffness, but it was one more thing she'd have to let slide for now.

When I have more of myself to give, if I ever have more of myself to give, we'll work on this.

"I want to visit the technician's home," she said, her eyes scanning the sidewalk ahead. A sea of people moved past, eyes down and lost to their internal lenscapes. Eyes glowed blue with the active light from their lenses. One man danced and bobbed to a rhythm only he could hear. "We don't have a search and seizure, but I suspect that maybe we won't need one."

"Why?" Heron asked. Despite their difference in height, he was being careful to stay beside her as they walked.

"On the elevator ride down, I looked up his address and information. He has a woman living with him, and they have a pending marriage application."

"A fiancée?" Heron asked with an air of gossip.

"Hopefully we'll catch her at home."

Another cacophony of beeps and chirps sounded, but Grace realized that it wasn't another fancy gadget stowed away on Heron's person. It was her calorie watch.

They both lifted and turned their calorie watches at the

same moment. Hers was half torn at the strap. Its face was scratched from where her body, blown by the blast, had skidded along the concrete. It was no surprise to her that his was the latest model.

He smiled. "Lunch first?"

THEY CHOSE A FUSION BISTRO THREE BLOCKS FROM RAVEE'S apartment. Grace slid into the cool booth, and Heron mirrored her. They tapped their watches against the sensor plate affixed to the wall and waited for checkmark confirmation that all of their food preferences, allergies, tastes, and caloric needs were recorded.

Then the embedded menu in the tabletop lit up, and the screen before them changed, showing a variety of dishes the restaurant offered that would satisfy those needs and preferences.

Grace selected a dumpling soup first, and the menu suggested she add the leaf-wrapped veggies in order to better fulfill her fiber needs. She acquiesced.

Heron selected a cheeseburger and fried green tomatoes on the side. Then the menus disappeared and they were left to each other.

"Do you know that meat used to come from animals?" he said companionably, drumming his fingers on the tabletop. "There were huge farms with thousands of acres where the animals were crammed in. So much land and water waste. It was horrible for the environment. Not to mention the slaughter—so not too good for the animals either. This was before the Land Conservation Act of 2380, of course."

Grace couldn't imagine a world where land, so costly and precious now, would be so poorly managed. She supposed it helped that they had less than ten billion people living on the planet then, compared to the 32.3 billion they had now. Not to mention they had had thousands more acres of usable land, having been yet untouched by rising seas and storm surges.

Heron was still talking. "I don't know how they ate it. Natural meat is absolutely *filthy*. Blood, shit, bacteria. Give me sterile lab-grown meat any day."

"You're full of information," Grace said, silently pulling up the photo she'd captured in the lab and surveying the faces again. She paid less attention to Ravee this time and more to the other Viscosity workers.

"Yes, well, my mother was a history professor. If you didn't hear forty historical facts at the dinner table, then you knew she was feeling rather morose that day. She was prone to it. Morosity. And spouting historical facts."

"I didn't know that Dr. Jane taught history."

"Oh, she didn't. I'm talking about Nora. Dr. Nora Avignon. I have two mothers."

Grace couldn't really focus on what he was saying. Her eye kept snagging on the photo hanging in her lenscape. She counted again.

"You have a look of consternation on your face, Commander. Can I ask what you're looking at?"

"There are sixty people in this photo."

"What photo?"

"I captured the photo from lab fourteen. Dr. Cyrah said fifty-eight people worked in the lab, but there are sixty people in this photo."

"I've received the list of all the lab workers we requested."

Her mailbox pinged. "Me too. Can you pair the faces with the names to see who's on the list? I want to know who these two mystery people are."

"Yes, yes," he said, and for the first time all day, since

she'd seen him flirting with the receptionist in the lobby of Viscosity Inc., he seemed truly engaged in the task at hand. "It shouldn't take more than a few minutes. Do you mind if I—"

"Go ahead," she said. She'd appreciate a moment to think to herself.

He sank into silence, his eyes slightly turned away from hers, using his lenscape to run the program as she asked. His eyes lit blue.

Grace took the chance to scan the restaurant. She noticed the people, bodies relaxed, and their soft conversations. Beyond that, the crowd walked back and forth past the bright window, sunbrellas up.

This wasn't so bad because she had never eaten in this restaurant with Davion or Kaiden. There were no memories here to rise up suddenly and squeeze her heart like a fist.

She could experience the place with her melancholy and her loss, but also without the loving grief suffocating her.

I'll have to abandon all our old haunts, she thought. *At least for a while.*

The Thai place in Low Town.

Pizza Palace on Forty-Second.

Kaiden's favorite creamery two blocks from their neighborhood.

A memory surfaced of Kaiden rushing ahead on his hoverskates as she trailed behind, her hand in Davion's. He was prattling on about something, but she didn't remember what it was. Work maybe. She'd been distracted by an identity theft case, someone trying to forge visas. Davion had been trying to take her mind off of it.

At least she would still have her favorite restaurant,

Sindu Serves. She'd eaten there mostly alone during the workday, and neither Davion nor Kaiden liked spicy food.

But there was *something* about this restaurant that unsettled her. She glanced around, wondering.

It was all the smiling.

No, it was also the calm.

That's how it had been at the precinct that night. A lot of smiling. A blanket of calm.

Before the IED exploded and tore her life apart.

The winter parade had sent a storm of red and green streamers through the air. Sparks of light danced past the precinct's pavilion. Grace had stood there with Davion's arm draped around her shoulder and Kaiden leaning his weight against her front as the dancers weaved in and out of the marching band.

The holographic circus was next. From where she stood, she saw the sparkling elephants and dolphins coming up the street.

The music, the cheers engulfed them. The smell of roasting nuts soaked in cinnamon and syrup hung in the air. Davion led Kaiden over to the street vendor and bought him a paper cone of them, slick with oil.

That's when Grace's lenscape had flared.

That's when she turned toward the precinct and saw the red X tapping out its warning, consuming her vision with its urgency. She'd run toward the entrance, toward the danger and—

A cork on a bottle of champagne popped, and Grace jumped, her knee hitting the underside of the table.

Heron looked up. "You all right?"

"Yeah." She was saved from explaining because the wall slot at the end of the table opened, and their orders slid onto the table.

Grace lifted her spoon, a slight tremor in her hand. She

reached for her lettuce wraps, peeling back the bamboo paper encasing them.

They ate in silence. Heron ate without regarding his food, clearly immersed in his task. The cheeseburger sat untouched in front of him as he slid a fried tomato into his mouth.

She forked a dumpling.

With Heron's attention distracted, she was able to fully survey him with all the scrutiny of a seasoned detective.

He had black hair that cut across his cheekbones in the current fashion. His eyes were a deep blue green, the color of the Tahitian Ocean. His nose was narrow, almost too small for his face, giving him a feminine look. The jaw was strong, but the cheeks were soft. The face was symmetrical except for the scar over one eyebrow. She wondered how he'd gotten it but would never ask.

He wasn't rugged as Davion had been. *Pretty* was more accurate, at least in regard to his face. But his body itself couldn't be mistaken for feminine. He had broad shoulders and tapering hips. The swell of a firm chest.

His appearance didn't have the ethereal gleam of a filter, so Grace suspected this was his real face, rather than a lenscape projection.

He was speaking again.

She blinked, coming out of her assessment to find those Tahitian eyes looking directly into hers. The refracted blue light of an active lenscape was gone.

"Excuse me?" she asked.

He popped another tomato chip into his mouth. "I said, Tomas Lake and Sam Crate. Those are the two from the photo. May I?"

Before she could answer, her lenscape pinged with the *<<accept lens share with heronjane1?>>*

She accepted, and her lenscape was overtaken by their

shared reality. The photo hung between them. Two faces were framed by blinking boxes. Then those faces enlarged and filled the scape side by side.

Heron, little more than a mirage in her vision now, wiped his mouth. "That is Lake on the left and Crate on the right. They aren't listed as employees in Viscosity's public roster, but the faces match tourist visas granted years ago."

"How long ago?"

"Four years ago for Lake. Six for Crate."

The group photo was replaced by two public IDs, confirming Heron's assessment.

"Maybe they were past employees?"

"Not listed," he said. "And interestingly, I can't find any information on them from their home zones either. On their visa applications it says Crate came from Zone 9 and Lake from Zone 168. But there are no histories of either in those zones."

"You shouldn't be able to access those zones' networks without formal permission and clearance," she said. "That would be a breach in security as well as treason."

He flashed a tight smile. "That's probably why I couldn't find anything."

"Why would they be in the photo if they weren't past or present employees? I doubt Viscosity welcomes tourists in from the street for photo opportunities."

"Either they were fired and removed from the record of employment—"

"Which is illegal and a violation of our tax and immigration treaties," Grace interjected.

"—or they quit," he finished.

"Dr. Cyrah said this was taken during an instructional seminar. Maybe they were in the building for something else? A conference"

"No, I checked. It was a private event. And even so, why would they be invited into the photo if they weren't employees."

"Strange," she said.

"Perhaps they were someone's dates," Heron suggested with a shrug.

Grace forked another dumpling. "What are their marital statuses?"

"Lake is single. But maybe he dated a lab employee. Crate has a wife."

"Does she work at Viscosity?" she asked. Of course, it wasn't unheard of for spouses to live in different zones if their visas were denied. If the job paid well enough, sometimes one of the pair would travel alone.

"No, she's another ghost. No record of her beyond a tourist visa processed the same time as Crate's. But there's a woman who looks just like her in an advertisement for one of the vertical farms in High Town. They also took hold after the Land Act," he added.

"Wives?" Grace asked, confused.

"No, sorry. The vertical farms. It was an excellent solution for saving land and protecting crops from volatile, unstable weather conditions. By moving our food indoors and building up we eliminated most crop loss. Every plant is logged and scanned and grows in its own individual container under the perfect conditions. It's given whatever it needs, not unlike Viscosity's organs. These microadjustments improved yield by nearly three thousand percent. Did you know they used to treat fields as a whole, nearly no individual attention was given to the plants. Something like a dry spell or pests rolled through and whole fields were lost. But now we can—"

"What does the wife have to do with this?" she asked gently.

"I'm sorry. I'm rambling again," he said with a sigh. "I'm saying that the wife's situation is similar to Lake's and Crate's. I think she has some connection to the High Town farm, but there is no record of her. Not publicly, anyway. I could look other places."

Grace wondered how often she could count on her new assistant to spout unsolicited information or suggest that he'd tried illegal tactics to retrieve information . . .

At least now he had his cheeseburger in his mouth.

She took this opportunity to issue clear instructions. "I want you to investigate these two men and find out why they were in the photo and what connection they have to Viscosity. I want to add them to the suspect list. You can look into the wife too, if you really feel like there's a connection. But I think the men are the key."

"Along with the technician, Ravee?"

"Yes," she confirmed. "Though we might eliminate him soon."

The menu on the table lit up, sensing their lightening plates, and offered additional service. Grace requested a second water, which was automatically fed through the slot and onto the table for her. Confirming their satisfaction, their accounts were deducted the price of the meals.

Grace noted the transaction confirmation in her lenscape and the faint *Goldstar Meals: Making Life Delicious* advertisement banner scrolling by.

"Will you continue your investigation of those two while we travel to Ravee's?" she asked.

"Already on it."

Which explained his look of quiet contemplation as they exited the restaurant and moved east toward the closest CityRide stop. Grace handled calling the auto, providing the server with their intended destination and fielding all the perfunctory, *would you like* questions.

Heron remained silent.

It was nice.

Grace liked his presence. She didn't realize until this moment that it was nice to have someone close, but without the expectation of engaging them.

It was something she had counted on Davion for. His reassuring silence, his companionship, without demands.

The complete absence of Davion and Kaiden had stunned her, but not enough that she'd wanted to invite over friends or relatives who would hover around her, their guilt pressing against her like a blanket over her face. Heavy.

Her best friend, Joleen, would've been perfect for the job. She knew how to be present and silent, just like this. But Joleen was on a military assignment and wouldn't make contact with the civilized world for another three months at least. How would she even begin to tell Joleen that Davion and Kaiden were gone?

A problem for another day.

The CityRide pulled off the main thoroughfare and into one of the residential neighborhoods. The buildings halved in size once, then again as they moved farther and farther from the city's thrumming center.

The neighborhoods, zoned for noise reduction and nature prevalence, were quieter and greener by design. The units themselves, enshrined in foliage and rose-gold solar panels, looked sleepy and contented in the early afternoon.

Grace thought Heron was deep into his research, comparing public data on their two new suspects. But then his eyes flicked up to hers and he said, "Did you know that natural trees produce pollen, seeds, and fruit?"

"No. I did not." The CityRide slowed to account for the reduced residential speed.

"All urban trees are modified to produce more oxygen, as well as absorb more carbon dioxide and particulate matter. And they don't produce any pollen. In fact, reproduction of any kind isn't possible. But if you visit the outer zones, you'll find only natural trees."

"Are the outer zones worried the trees will breed unchecked?" she asked, feeling as though she had a clear sense of what dinner must've been like in Heron's childhood home.

"No." He laughed. "No, I don't think that's a problem."

The CityRide stopped outside a small unit enshrined in thick green foliage, and large windows meant to let in as much natural light as possible.

"This is it," Grace said and was the first to exit the cool auto and step into the warm afternoon.

The walk connecting the street to the door was short but well maintained. No doubt Heron could tell her why if she asked. But he was all business now as he leaned forward and pressed the call button on the front of Ravee's housing unit.

It was a couple's unit, about half the size of Grace's own home, which was family sized. She supposed she should downgrade soon, since it was only her now.

Her throat tightened unexpectedly at an idea that had never occurred to her before—that she might lose her home as well as her family—so that when the door to the unit opened and a beautiful, dark-eyed woman answered, Grace found she couldn't speak.

Heron didn't miss a beat. "Good morning, Ms.—"

"He's dead, isn't he? Oh god, he's dead!" the woman blurted. The words seemed to leap from her throat as if they couldn't be held back any longer.

"Who?" Heron asked, alarmed. He leaned back from the woman as if she might leap on him.

Grace noticed her puffy eyes and flushed face. Finally, her voice returned to her. "Are you all right?"

The woman seemed to gain an ounce of control over herself then. She touched her braids as her gold eyeliner ran from the corners of her eyes.

"You're the police, aren't you? You came to tell me Ravee is dead?"

"No," Grace said. "We came to ask you questions."

"Do you know where Ravee is? He didn't come home last night, and he isn't answering any of my pings."

"May we come in?" Heron asked gently, and Grace saw the way the other woman reacted to him. "You're Risa Shou, correct?"

"Yes," she said, dabbing at her eyes. Gold stained her fingers.

"We came by because you're listed as engaged to marry Ravee. You are also his emergency contact." Grace added.

"What's happened?" she cried

"We aren't sure. But we'd like to tell you what we know if you let us come in and ask you some questions."

Finally, Risa opened the door wider and let them into the unit. They followed her down a pristine hallway to the kitchen on the right. They all took their seats around a legless table that sat suspended off the ground. The legless, backless seats were also suspended.

The magnetic plate must be under the rug, Grace thought.

"Would you like anything to drink?" Risa asked, rubbing her nose with a tissue that she produced from her pocket.

"No, thank you," Grace said.

"I would love some tea. You have Earl Grey?"

Risa looked surprised. "I do."

"Lemon?" Heron asked.

"Yes."

He folded his fingers and smiled. "Perfect."

She looked relieved to have something to do with her hands besides wringing them. "Did you go by Viscosity?"

"We did. We're interviewing employees about a theft that occurred last night."

Her eyebrows shot up in alarm. "You think Ravee stole something?"

"We can't possibly know until we speak to him," Grace said immediately. "Have you seen him?"

"No, but he can't talk about work," Risa said, dipping the kettle beneath the sink's faucet to fill. "They've all signed nondisclosure agreements. He won't even talk to me."

"So you wouldn't be able to tell us what he is working on?" Heron probed gently.

"I would ask questions but he would always refuse to answer them. When he didn't come home last night, I thought maybe he was held up at work. Sometimes Dr. Cyrah keeps him late."

A vacuuming robot slid along the floor. Grace lifted her legs to oblige it. "When was the last time you saw Ravee?"

"Yesterday morning, as he was getting ready for work. I was making breakfast when he said he had to go in early to meet a coworker."

"Did you hear from him after? Maybe on a break or . . ."

"No. Nothing." She poured dried leaves in the basket and pulled a knife for the lemon from the drawer. "It's unlike him. That's why when I didn't hear back, I kept trying to send messages. But they aren't going through. I called Viscosity, but they won't speak to me."

"I suspect they won't speak to anyone until the investigation concludes," Heron said.

Risa grimaced. "No, they've refused my calls before. Dr. Cyrah even hung up on me. More than once."

She put the tea in front of Heron, its steaming cup balanced on its delicate saucer. A bright lemon slice hung from the rim.

Heron squeezed the yellow rind and dropped it into the dark tea. He inhaled the steam deeply. "Ah, yes. Very nice. I can already tell this is going to be *very* good."

This compliment earned a small smile from Risa. But it was gone the second she turned back to Grace. "You didn't see him, did you? When you went to interview people about the theft?"

"No," Grace admitted. She didn't want to add to the woman's distress, but pretending as if she didn't know anything would only agitate her further. She wasn't stupid. "I was told he didn't come in for his shift this morning."

"No, *no*." Risa stood and turned a full circle, pacing around them at the kitchen table. "Something's happened."

<<Accept private chat with heronjane1?>>

Grace accepted.

<<It's unlikely that Ravee was working double morning and night shifts two days in a row, don't you think?>> he asked. His eyes remained fixed and sympathetic on the woman. The interior dialogue betrayed nothing.

<<Very,>>Grace agreed, refusing to look in his direction. <<It's possible he lied to her about his schedule.>>

<<Do you think she's killed him and hidden his body?>>

<<No. I think she's genuinely afraid for his life.>>

<<And there's no chance Risa can give us anything? Leads?>>

Leads. Grace thought. *What inspector spoke like that?*

Grace looked the woman over once, then let her eyes sweep over the immaculate kitchen and table.

<<No. If Ravee had something to hide, he wouldn't keep it here. She would find it.>>

The text box disappeared from her lenscape without Heron's reply.

"Sit down," he said gently to the pacing woman who'd resumed wringing her hands. "You're going to make yourself sick."

It was such a sweet, caring thing to say that it caught Grace by surprise. He'd seemed flippant and flirtatious at Viscosity. This true sincerity was a surprising contrast. Or he was a very good actor.

"If he didn't return home and didn't stay for a double shift, something has happened," Risa said, sinking into the kitchen chair. "What is happening to this zone? Is *anybody* safe anymore?"

Grace replayed Commander Adams's warning from that morning. *After what happened, people are scared.*

"Can you tell me what happened the last time you saw Ravee. Take us up until the moment when he left for work yesterday." The awkward curve of the seat was pressing into the back of Grace's legs. "Did he say anything strange? Do anything strange?"

Except for disappearing without a trace.

Risa sniffed again. "No, he kissed me and left."

"Did he seem upset or worried?" Heron jumped in.

"He seemed rushed," Risa said. "I assumed that something had happened at work. He's complained about how finicky the systems are. They lost thirteen organs last month due to a glitch in the computer. He was given a written warning by Dr. Cyrah. She threatened to fire him. He's been working very hard to stay on her good side since."

Out of the corner of her eye, Grace saw Heron shift in his seat. She pretended she didn't.

Fresh tears welled up in Risa's eyes. "This is how it happens, isn't it? One minute everything is fine and the next it isn't."

She turned her gaze on Grace, as if Grace knew the answer.

On the sunny little street outside Risa's unit, Grace moved to open her sunbrella but Heron shook his head. "The rating went down. You should be okay."

She slid the sunbrella pen into her pocket and began down the walkway.

After ten minutes, they reached the CityRide stop at the end of the residential block. The network bulletin pinged, informing her of the rating change.

"So what do you think?" Heron asked, rubbing his palms against his suit jacket.

"I think she's grieving," Grace replied. *And wouldn't I know what that looks like?* "She knows he's dead."

"Is he dead?" Heron asked, eyebrow cocked. "Men run off sometimes."

Women know, she thought. After all, hadn't it been her first thought upon waking in the hospital? *They're dead. Oh god, they're dead.*

The night of the explosion, at the precinct, she'd stood outside the storage closet in the small corridor where the public receiving area and private offices connected. The bomb detection program had kept flashing its red warning, telling her she was still within the blast radius.

Instead of running, she'd opened the closet and saw the IED on the floor, a square metal device, wedged between a bucket of cleaners and the mop and broom.

She'd sent two messages then. The first to her husband: <<Get Kaiden away from here. Now. There's a bomb in the precinct. Run! Run! Run!>>

<<Where the hell are you?>> had been his instant reply.

But she was already composing the second message, one that her privilege as commander afforded her.

She seized the lenscape of every officer on the network in an emergency override command.

<<This is Commander Buteo. There is an IED in the Zone 2 precinct building. Vacate the premises immediately. Clear the area at least three city blocks. Seek shelter. >>

She heard the outcry rise in the streets outside. The frantic scuffle of feet. The faltering music changing its rhythm.

<<Gray! >>Her husband pinged her again. But she was already bending down to place her hands on the strange box, her trembling fingers pinching and lifting wires. <<Gray, answer me now!>>

She never did fulfill his last request.

"Did you catch the bit about the lost organs?" Heron asked, placing his hands in his pockets.

Grace blinked against the memories and found herself on the sunny street again. She coughed, clearing her voice. "The question is whether or not those thirteen organs were destroyed by a failing computer or stolen. The failing computer story could've been a cover."

She summoned an auto and gave it their location, accepting the convenience surcharge that came with not meeting the auto at a designated auto stop.

"Do you think Ravee Kapur is running an organ

scam?" Heron asked. He shielded his eyes from the sun. "If he's not making enough as a Viscosity tech maybe he's selling organs on the side, to pay for a luxurious wedding, perhaps? I've heard there's good money in it."

"Where did you hear it's good money to sell organs?"

He smiled mischievously. "I don't remember."

She pressed on. "I don't know about the organ scam, but here are the questions I have so far. Why were Crate and Lake in that photograph? What is their connection to Viscosity? Do those two have a connection to Ravee? Where is Ravee, and does he share any responsibility? Why didn't Dr. Cyrah mention the organs lost last month or Lake and Crate? We need to interview her again."

"So are we adding Cyrah to the list of suspects then?"

"Everyone is a suspect. For all I know, you have a liver in each pocket."

"You're rather paranoid, aren't you?" Then he seemed to hear what he was saying. His smile fell. "Hell, of course you are. Why wouldn't you be paranoid? Sorry."

The entire mood of the conversation shifted, pulling silence over them like a cold mist.

Heron tried to escape the clammy discomfort of it. "Maybe Ravee wanted to present Risa with a heart. A *real* heart. People in love do strange things."

Grace saw the CityRide rolling up to the curb, and her shoulders relaxed. "We should call it a day. Or at least do our homework and reconvene later."

This was an excuse. The truth was she was tired. It was nearly two in the afternoon, and just six hours of work had been enough to exhaust her completely.

Be gentle with yourself, the discharge physician had said as he'd wheeled her out to the waiting CityRide that would take her home to an empty house and an empty life. *You'll need time before you're a hundred percent again.*

"Actually, do you mind calling yourself an auto?" she added. "I want to head home."

"Not at all," Heron said, but the forced cheerfulness showed. "I have more than enough to keep me busy tonight. Shall I call you if I discover anything?"

"Yes, please."

He gave her a mock salute and turned rather playfully on his heels, walking—presumably—in the direction of the next auto stop.

But there was nothing playful in his tense shoulders and quick stride.

As she climbed into the waiting auto, Grace wondered what expression he wore on his face.

FIVE

THE WHITE CITYRIDE auto returned Grace to her unit. Two bedrooms, a one-car garage, and a lawn large enough for children to play in awaited her. The exterior beamed golden with its collected sunlight.

The garage registered her biometric approach and opened for her.

It sat empty. No auto.

Because hers had been blown apart at the edge of the precinct's pavilion.

She supposed the precinct would issue her a new auto for her personal use if she requested one. But she didn't want it.

When she'd climbed into the CityRide, the hospital bracelet still on her wrist, her whole body had trembled. She had been convinced that somehow, whoever wanted her to die knew she was being discharged that day. Knew which CityRide she would get into and where to plant the device that would end her life.

That was ridiculous, of course. How many autos must zoom along the Zone 2 streets in a day?

It didn't matter that she was full of as much hope as fear at the prospect of dying. If she were killed, at least she wouldn't have to go on.

And yet she'd still been trembling when the auto rolled up to the front of her house, her mother waiting to receive her.

You're shaking all over! her mother had cried when she reached into the auto to help Grace's aching body out.

I'm cold, Grace had lied.

If Grace ordered a new private auto, she would certainly wonder *Is this it? Is this the day?* every time she climbed into it. She would climb inside and wait for the explosion that would end her life.

Grace pushed these thoughts away as she crossed the garage toward the door that led into the house. Her gaze slid automatically to the receiving platform in the far left corner: a two-by-three-meter slab that groaned as it opened to accept packages.

It sat empty today. No deliveries from the intricate tube system below.

"Welcome home, Grace," the AI announced as she stepped into the house. "Did you have a pleasant day?"

"I'm still here, aren't I?" she replied, wondering what sadist had programmed these bots.

"That's the spirit. You have one message from your mother. Would you like to hear it?"

"Sure."

Gracie, it's me. I came by today to see if you needed anything. I guess you really went to work. How did it go? Since you weren't home, I programmed your dinners for the week in the ChefMate. I chose eighteen hundred as the serving time because I thought you'd be home then. But if you're back at the precinct, you probably want it later. I know how you like to work late into the night. You're just like your father.

Anyway, call me before you go to bed or I'll call you at oh two hundred when I get up to see the Cup. It's Australia versus France. If you don't pick up, I'll leave a two-hour play-by-play. You'll love that.

The call cut off her snort of laughter, so Grace stood in her living room, ears ringing with it. Her mother would never make it to oh two hundred. Grace knew she'd call long before that.

Kicking off her shoes in the middle of the kitchen floor, she padded barefoot to the sofa and collapsed over the arm.

Her face hit the cushions first, and she groaned. She couldn't feel the scratchy fabric on the burned side. That's when she realized Risa hadn't stared at her scars. Her concern for Ravee must've been all-consuming.

How much of the world had she missed because of her own grief?

Grace rolled onto her back and placed one of the throw pillows under her head. For a long time, she only looked at the ceiling and thought nothing. It was a marvelous trick, and probably the only reason she was still alive. She was able to completely empty her head when she needed to.

But she couldn't sustain it for more than a few minutes before crushing anxiety rose up to meet her, amplified by the silence in the house.

No movement in the bedrooms above. Nor in the yard surrounding.

Only the sound of air leaving her lungs, slipping past her dry lips.

The blue light of her network responder caught her eye. *Your heart rate and blood pressure are elevated. Run CALM program?*

"No," Grace said to the ceiling, which was

programmed to look like the afternoon sky. Digital clouds that looked so real she honestly couldn't tell a difference except in one way: this digital sky was clearer. There was no haze as one could expect with the true sky.

"Replay memory eight twenty-eight."

Her lenscape changed, and the sky fell away. In its place, a memory unfurled, so fresh and real that she felt as if she were in the moment again.

We present Commander Grace Helena Buteo!

The hall boomed with whistles and cheers. Glasses chinked together. The heavy applause assaulted her from every direction as a large hand—Commander Adams's—touched her shoulder lightly.

"Congratulations," he whispered in her ear. His voice was a low rumble that she felt in her chest.

She turned and found her family standing on the side of the banquet hall stage.

Davion clapped furiously. His gaze was so intent that he'd sucked his bottom lip up with his teeth and pinned it there, turning the flesh white.

With a last wave, she exited the stage, and Davion threw his arms around her. He hugged her hard.

"I'm damn proud of my woman." His lips were soft on her ear. "*Damn* proud of you, Gray."

Clutching her leg, two small arms squeezed. She laughed, bent down, and scooped Kaiden into her arms.

Again that inward turning. Her desire to look away, keep herself from the heartbreak of Kaiden's face. His little body, now completely, totally gone from her. Forever.

When that long-ago version of herself had placed a hand on the top of Kaiden's head, he'd pulled it down and kissed it. The three of them had laughed.

But she didn't meet her son's gaze.

"You won, Mommy. You won!"

"She did win. We've all won," Davion said, squeezing her again. "There's no one better to keep this zone safe. They're right to believe in you."

Grace let the memory play as tears streamed from the corners of her eyes, unfelt over her ruined cheek. As she wrestled with the cowardice in her heart, she fell asleep to their voices.

Something woke her. She sat up on her sofa and found the room had darkened. The digital sky above had faded from a bright afternoon to the dim setting sun. This added an eerie silence. Long shadows stretched across the carpet and table.

Again, that soft whirring caught her ear. She turned, tracing the sound.

It was the ChefMate. Its long silver arm had slid from the storage slot in the wall above the stove and was now joined by its pair. It began working furiously over the stove, concocting whatever her mother had ordered for dinner. Pans rattled. The slight hiss of the heating element clicked on. Something was thrown into a pan. Fresh garlic and onion, by the smell of it.

As if on cue, the house phone rang.

"Buteo."

"Buteo?" Her mother snorted. "Heavens, Grace. You sound like a ruffian."

"What's for dinner?"

"Penne in a thick cream sauce and extra garlic and saffron. You're getting too skinny."

"How would you know?" She hadn't seen her mother in two weeks.

"I read your scale. Yesterday, you only weighed fifty-five kilos. That's too low, honey."

"Then you shouldn't have given me your metabolism."

"Don't sauce me. You know what I mean. It's normal to lose weight when you're grieving, but don't go too far."

"With crème penne, I'm sure I won't."

"Eat the damned noodles. Oh, and I ordered ice cream for dessert. Three servings. Just in case."

"In case of what?"

"The house is still programmed for three. You won't get hit with an extra sugar tax."

Grace pinched the bridge of her nose and took a deep breath. "I appreciate your concern, Mom. Really."

"You should. It's free of charge. Anyway, forget it. How was your first day back? Tell me they didn't give you anything difficult. As if you don't deserve a full pension for the rest of your life for what you've sacrificed."

"Some organs were stolen," she said.

"Hell's bells," her mother swore. "What can someone do with those? This isn't another one of those Frankenstein scandals, is it?"

"No. I don't think so." Grace remembered the report from Zone 6. A scientist had lost his wife in the super flu outbreak five years ago. He'd tried to clone her, thinking he could simply add her memories from a stored bank and it would be like having her again. Unfortunately, full-body human cloning was illegal. He was arrested before his project was complete, and his new wife was destroyed.

"Then why do they need so many parts?"

"I don't know yet."

Her mother harrumphed. "This is certainly better than I hoped. I was worried they'd have you writing sun tickets, and that would've really sent you off the deep end."

"What is *the deep end* exactly?"

"I don't know. Going after the bomber."

The bomber. Grace's throat tightened. Her heart pounded in her ears. "I don't want to see him."

"Good," her mother replied. "I don't want you anywhere *near* someone like that. It's bad enough that I lost Davion and Kaiden. If I lost you too—"

You lost them? You? It required conscious effort to relax her jaw.

"Your dinner is ready, Grace," the ChefMate announced, pulling a white dish from the cabinet and pouring her creamed noodles into the bowl. "Would you like cheese and parsley garnish?"

"Say yes," her mother instructed.

"Yes," Grace replied, knowing it was best to pick her battles. She climbed from the sofa and went to retrieve her food.

The ChefMate obeyed. "Your meal has been logged. Thank you for trusting ChefMate with your dietary needs. ChefMate. The affordable in-home chef so you have more time for what matters."

For what matters. She wasn't sure what mattered anymore.

Her mother sighed. "I hate that they have to recite their pitch at every meal. I swear, I wake up in the dead of night, hungry and thinking, 'ChefMate, the in-home chef, *vah, vah, vah . . .*'"

"I suspect that's the idea," Grace said, taking the bowl and fork and moving to the table. "Subliminal advertising, isn't it? If your friend asks for a recommendation for the best home chef, they want 'ChefMate' to roll right off your tongue."

"Turn on the video. I want to see your face."

"No, you want to see if I really eat this."

"Come on," her mother said, and Grace's lenscape was pinged with <<*share video with CarolinaCaroline89?*>>

Grace sighed and accepted the request.

Her mother's bright smile greeted her. She was at her own kitchen table, poised like a duchess, her long lashes curled up coquettishly. A sweater hung off one shoulder, revealing sharp collarbones. She'd done her lips in a bright red. She looked fifty, not ninety-two. She suspected the natural filter helped.

"Lovely," her mother said. "Look at you. You're getting your color back. Are you sleeping more?"

"Yes," she answered truthfully. Last night was the first night she'd gotten four hours straight without waking prematurely, heart pounding to the sound of metal crunching in her ears. But she wasn't prepared to tell her mother about the crutch she was using to get her to sleep.

Replaying memories of her dead husband wouldn't be considered *healthy* behavior.

"Take a bite for Momma," Caroline teased. Her light-colored hair lay sleek over her shoulders. Her eyebrows were drawn dark today.

Grace rolled her eyes and shoved a large bite of penne into her mouth.

Her mother laughed. It was a halfhearted sound. And just that tonal shift warned Grace of what was coming. She sucked in a breath, bracing herself.

"Gracie, how are you *really*?"

"How do you think I am?" Grace asked, shoving the penne in her mouth. She hoped overloading one sense would dampen another. Or she would choke on her food as well as cry.

"Devastated," her mother said, releasing another tense sigh. "I wish I knew what to do for you."

"You've done plenty."

"It's not the same as when your father died. That wasn't a surprise. I mean eighty-eight years old is young, but he'd been fighting *C. auris* for a long time. It wasn't sudden. No one should have to survive a loss like yours. To get up day after day after losing a child—my god. If I'd lost you when you had the flu, I don't know what I would've done. A daughter dead at thirteen. I can't imagine it."

A son dead at eight.

It wasn't just Kaiden, she wanted to say. Losing Kaiden might have broken her on its own, absolutely. But at least she would have had Davion to help her through. Her best friend. The only one who could surprise a laugh out of her. The one who pulled her back when she went too hard, pressed too far into herself, into the world, into her work. He reminded her that the inhale was as important as the exhale. The rest was as important as the work.

But she'd lost them both. Her earth and her sky. Now her world was groundless. Empty.

"At least you got fifteen good years with Davion," her mother was saying.

Grace made an inarticulate sound that could be taken for agreement.

"I'm sure you're sick of hearing it, but I'm sorry," she said. "I'm sorry that your pathetic excuse for a mother can't do more for you."

"Don't be ridiculous."

"I'm your mother. I'm supposed to know how to help you. Maybe it's because I didn't carry you myself."

"Mom, stop. You're being crazy right now."

Grace rose from the table and got a glass of water to wash down the rich pasta dish. It was very good. And if her mother hadn't ordered it, she supposed she would have likely skipped dinner altogether.

"I would've carried you if I could have," she said. "Damn uterine torsion."

"You know there is no correlation between artificial womb incubation and mother–child attachment."

"At least you got to carry Kaiden. You got *that*."

The penne soured in Grace's mouth.

"I'm sorry," her mother said. "I'm making it about me again. What a shit thing to do."

Grace took a drink of water—slowly, methodically—before she said, "Forget about it, Mom. Let's just talk about something else."

"What's there to talk about?"

"You?" Grace offered, knowing her mother could hardly resist. "How are you?"

"Not bad. It's nice to be back with Henry. And the new Koda Jones book dropped today. *In Her Darkest Dreams.* Have you read it?"

"No."

"Me neither. Henry's kept me busy."

Grace choked. "Mom. I don't need to know."

"He missed me, if you know what I'm saying."

As disturbing as the image of her mother astride her robot companion may have been, Grace couldn't stop it from rising in her mind unbidden. Her recently replaced hips, working furiously to grind the creature into the unyielding mattress.

Grace pinched the bridge of her nose. "What happens between you and Henry should stay between you and Henry."

"Maybe that's what you need," her mother offered. "You can get a Boi made to look just like Davion."

"*No*, Mother." Grace's stomach turned. "I don't think that will fool anyone. Least of all *me*. And seeing the robot will just remind me he's dead." *As if I could forget.*

"You're so young. Forty-three is nothing. I met your father at forty-six. You can remarry and have more children if you want. I was forty-nine when I had you. So many women are having children in their sixties and seventies now. It's trendy."

That was the farthest possibility from Grace's mind, but it was another one of those comments she let slide by.

"I dated for a while after your father died."

"I remember. There was that Portuguese futboller."

"Oh yes, he was *handsome*. But so young."

Grace was pretty sure her mother preferred men young.

"Adams is still single. He *is* a handsome man," her mother went on. "And he came to see you when you were hurt. Unless you'd like to try women? I dated a woman for a while before your father."

"The artist, I remember." Her mother would tell anyone who listened about her days posing as a naked muse for an art major. "Why do you want me to date when you can't even be bothered yourself?"

"You're right. People can be tiresome."

Like the one I'm talking to.

"Robots just do what they're told. It's wonderful. The first companion I made was modeled after your father. That was a mistake. Why look back when you can have better? I know some people program them to clean and run errands, but we both know what I wanted him for."

"Mother, *please*."

"Dessert is in the box, Grace," the ChefMate declared.

Her mother prattled on. "I suppose Davion was very good in bed. He looked it—"

"Mom, for the love of all."

Davion, in fact, had been very good in bed. He was an attentive and enthusiastic lover. But Grace would die before she said so.

"Not like Davion then," her mother said, her voice

gaining excitement. "How about something else? Do you have a celebrity crush or an old secret flame or—"

<<Accept call from heronjane1?>>

"Hold on. I have a call."

Her mother's face was cut off midstream and replaced with Heron's. It startled her to see those water-colored eyes so close to her own. The intimacy made her stomach drop. He seemed stunned as well. For a moment, his gaze only regarded her, searching her face, speechless. Then he managed to say, "What are you doing?"

"Eating." She tilted her bowl so that he could see. "What's happened?"

He blinked. The focus returned to his eyes. "They've found Ravee."

"Does he have the organs?" she asked, sitting up taller at the kitchen table.

"No. He doesn't have anything. Not even a pulse."

"He's dead."

Risa's tearstained face sprang to mind. Grace pushed her bowl away.

"They've quarantined the lab where they found him. But I don't know how long they plan to comply with us."

"He's *at* Viscosity?"

"Yes."

"Where are you now?" she asked. She was already up and searching for her shoes. She found them on the floor where she'd kicked them off. One lay dejected on its side.

"Home," he said.

"Ping me the address and I'll pick you up. I'm on my way now."

He hung up first, and her mother's face returned full form to the lenscape.

"I have to go. Our suspect just turned up dead."

Her mother wrinkled her nose. "Finish your dinner first. Come on. Let me see."

Grace obediently shoveled the last three bites into her mouth and tipped the bowl up for her mother's approval.

"Good girl. And excellent timing. Look, it's Henry."

Just past her mother's shoulder, the AI appeared. His perfectly sculpted body stood fully nude. Erect.

Grace terminated the call without saying goodbye.

SIX

GRACE GAVE the CityRide auto Heron's address and wasn't surprised to soon find herself in one of the city's premier bio-sealed communities. When the CityRide paused at the entrance, a message appeared on her lenscape.

Hello, Commander Buteo. You have been granted access to Sunrise Ridge for twenty-four hours as the guest of Mr. Heron Jane. Please enjoy your stay at Sunrise Ridge. Sunrise. The best part of your day.

How the system recognized her by her lenscape ID alone was a question for another day. Grace was too busy gawking at the size of the houses and the water feature weaving between the units. The solar lights were a soft rose gold, and the street itself was made of the same absorbent material. The residents could enjoy as much energy and water consumption as they were willing to pay for. Must be nice.

The CityRide rolled to a stop in front of unit 44.

Grace exited the auto and found Heron stepping out of the unit. Her steps faltered on the walkway.

She had to admit to herself she was a little disappointed. Her curiosity was certainly piqued, and she wanted to see inside his home. Heron wore expensive clothes and digital accessories that must have cost her entire salary, but what did it look like inside his house?

Did he like art? Did he cook or did he have a chef? Did he have plants or a pet?

She found herself building a personality profile for one Heron Jane as he stood on the porch, adjusting his sleeve.

Then another man stepped out of the house behind him and shut the door.

A short, flirtatious exchange flew between the two as Grace tried to take in every detail of the stranger's appearance. Tall, sandstone skin, and black eyes. Long black hair that hung between his shoulder blades.

He lightly placed a kiss on Heron's lips and then started down the walk toward her.

He flashed a charming smile. As he waved hello, she saw the red-ink tattoo on the side of his middle finger. "Good evening."

"Hello," she managed before he slid into the waiting auto.

When she turned around, Heron was smiling down at her. "Arjun needs a ride to the stop. Is that okay?"

"Sure," she said, because what else could she say to such a request?

"Great," he said. "I'll get the auto." And before she could protest, he was already offering the CityRide his payment details and travel request.

Grace and Heron climbed in after Arjun and said nothing. Grace sat on one bench, with Heron and Arjun opposite her. Arjun smiled, secretly, his eyes fixed somewhere on the houses outside his window. When Arjun and

Heron smiled reflexively at the same moment, Grace knew they shared a private chat.

Unwilling to discuss the case in front of a stranger, Grace embraced the silence. She scanned the auto's interior, the passing buildings, and the scenery as if they mattered. She distracted herself with anything but the two men sharing an intimate moment in front of her. It reminded her of the way she felt with Lore Duchovny.

He often kissed his wife so passionately at some of the precinct's events, Grace knew she was not the only one who found the display uncomfortable.

And Heron and Arjun weren't even touching.

The auto slid to a stop. "We have arrived at your destination, Mr. Jane. Your account has been debited nine dollars. Thank you for using CityRide."

Arjun briefly squeezed Heron's leg, just above the knee, before stepping out onto the bright street. At the last moment, he ducked his head back inside and gave Grace a wide grin, teeth gleaming. "It was nice to meet you, Commander."

The door closed before she fully recovered.

"I have another stop," Heron told the CityRide. "Viscosity Inc., please."

"There is a four-minute delay due to level-one traffic."

"That's fine," Heron replied, his eyes meeting Grace's as if offering her the chance to interject. She only inclined her head.

"Would you like me to play from your playlist, Mr. Jane?" the auto asked.

"No, thank you. I would like silence so I can speak with my friend."

The auto obeyed, and Grace was left looking into those Tahitian-blue waters.

"Arjun is a prostitute," she blurted.

Heron's lips quirked to the corner. "I'm aware."

She wasn't sure how to follow this announcement, seeing again in her mind's eye the red tattoo of the sex worker imprinted on the tender flesh of his middle finger.

"Sex work is legal, Commander."

"Of course it's legal."

"I was at home when you picked me up."

"Right."

His eyebrows arched, amused. "It is because Arjun is a man?"

"No."

"Perhaps I'm not as great a detective as you," he said, that smile deepening. His shoulders shifted against the seat as if he was settling in. "*Why* does it matter that a male sex worker was at my house?"

"It doesn't."

"Ah," he said, and his face looked as though he was working hard to suppress a laugh. "Now that that's settled, can I tell you what I learned about Ravee Kapur?"

She hesitated. Her mind kept circling back to the words *sex worker*.

If it didn't matter—and it didn't—why couldn't she let it go? Was it that he was a sex worker and not a husband or a longtime lover? Was it that Heron was very attractive and surely had no need to *pay* for attention? Did it bother her to learn he was the noncommittal type? Perhaps he preferred affection on demand with no precursor or expectation.

Give it up, Gray, she told herself. *Your own mother sleeps with a robot.*

Maybe that was it. Maybe Heron preferred the convenience of a robot, but with a beating heart.

"I can see this is bothering you," Heron said.

"No. You're right. Sex work is perfectly respectable,"

she said, perhaps too quickly. "But you didn't tell him anything about the case, did you?"

The amusement disappeared at once. "Did I give you the impression I don't know how to conduct an investigation?"

Yes, actually, she realized. But seeing Arjun hadn't had much to do with that. It was a slow accumulation of small, overlookable offenses.

He looked out the window and seemed to consider something for a long moment. Then in a complete shift of mood he said, "I think better during sex."

She coughed, choking on the spit in her mouth.

His amused grin returned in full form. "Maybe the act sends extra blood to my brain."

"I don't—" But she couldn't even finish. *I don't think it works that way* seemed like an invitation to discuss the mechanics of sex.

Heron seemed oblivious to her embarrassment or the heat burning her face. "I was trying to piece together what we knew so far. I invited Arjun over to assist me."

"Inspector, whatever happens in your free time is your business. I don't need to—"

"I just wanted to assure you that I am committed to the case. I'm fully invested in uncovering the truth," he said, his gaze unwavering. "No matter how many *hours* it takes."

He's screwing with me, she thought. She felt her tight, scarred face twitch in an involuntary smile. "All right, enough. I get your point."

He seemed triumphant. His posture relaxed against the seat again. "Ravee Kapur was found dead in one of the laboratories adjacent to lab fourteen. I was told that it's little more than a glorified storage cabinet, which is why no one went in there until the janitor arrived for her shift. The coroner is already there. They put the time of death at around oh one hundred."

"So he died last night."

"Correct," Heron said, fussing with the amplifier ring.

"We need to know who else was in the building at the time. I'd prioritize whoever was on the same floor. Though I suspect floors can be crossed in minutes, so I'm not sure how much that really matters. Any progress with Crate and Lake?"

"No," he said, looking truly sorry. "There are some mysteries surrounding that."

"Tell me."

"They have no employment histories, which is odd. Their addresses were current until eight months ago, when it looks like they were removed from the system. Now their previous homes are owned by other people. Lake, in fact, used to live in my neighborhood."

"Where do they live now?"

"They have no other addresses listed in this zone."

"Is it possible they moved out of zone?"

"It's possible, but if they applied for a change of status, it should show up in their records. But there are no immigration records. I sent a cross-network request to be sure. It's possible that someone got lazy with the paperwork. But immigration would have certainly recorded them if they'd moved to a new zone. Even on tourist visas."

Why would they purge all their information from the network? Grace wondered.

To better commit a crime. Like Lix Richards.

Viscosity Inc. rolled into sight. White birds circled the top of the building, their underbellies bright as they searched for a place to land.

Grace exited the auto first as Heron settled up with the CityRide. Before they even reached Viscosity's gleaming doors, the receptionist appeared, moving toward them expectantly. She had her arms crossed over the front of her body, her back curving into a C.

Heron was the first to speak to her. "Thank you so much for calling."

"He's really dead." She looked ready to throw herself against Heron's chest. Fortunately, she did not. "He's *really* dead."

Grace's thought of Risa again. Her red-rimmed eyes, puffy and dark. The tremble that had seized her lips.

She didn't want to return to Risa's house and confront the woman's grief. It was like cutting her nail to the quick.

"I've been asked to bring you up to the lab. Please follow me." The receptionist turned and led them toward the elevators.

Dutifully, they followed her through the lobby, past the large screens playing Viscosity adverts on repeat. They took the elevator up to the same lab where they'd visited Dr. Cyrah.

When they stepped off the elevator, Grace realized they were last to the party.

Many of her coworkers were already on the scene, dissecting the room and all its contents.

Grace found her eyes scanning the coats expectantly, looking to see if anyone had picked up any evidence accidentally. But the sensory coats remained pristine.

Two officers stood over Ravee Kapur's corpse, photographing evidence with their lenscapes for the archive. All collected evidence was to be compiled and organized into a single case file by the system. They scanned the area to detect everything from blood tracks to fingerprints and other clues that could give them a clearer picture of what had happened here. Grace would assess the data and divide the tasks when she got back to the precinct and completed a manual review of their findings.

Murder investigations, as rare as they were, made sure no one got home at a decent hour. She found a bit of gratitude in knowing that she would not have to call Davion and disappoint him for not making it home in time for dinner, homework, or bedtime.

But how would that disappointment even compare to how she'd already failed him?

Someone called her name. Grace looked up and found a friendly face in the crowd.

Forensics cataloguer Juke Yin leaned over Kapur's corpse, waving Grace over.

Grace excused herself through the throng of bodies, accepting clear protective covers for her shoes and gloves for her hands from the tech who offered them. She gloved up first, then, leaning on a bare spot of wall, slipped the covers over each of her shoes.

"You don't look happy," Grace said, stopping short of the blood in which Yin stood. A thick suction sound slurped every time she lifted her foot.

Yin gave her a wan smile of acknowledgment. "And to think my mother wanted me to be a podiatrist."

"Mine was hoping for a famous climatologist or DDS programmer. What happened?" She bent down, her face in profile to Yin's.

"He was struck on the back of the head with something hard enough to cave in his skull," Yin replied plainly. "If that didn't kill him on the spot, he soon bled to death, as you can tell."

Grace could tell. There was far too much blood on the floor.

"But nothing in this room matches the markings. They must've taken the weapon with them. The judge just approved a search and seizure, but it's going to take a long time to sweep a building of this size, and there's no guarantee that the weapon is *in* the building anymore. Not to mention the fact that Dr. Cyrah is two steps from hysterical. She claims we are compromising the integrity of her lab, *vah, vah, vah.* She's making me nervous with all her pacing."

"What kind of weapon are we looking for?" Heron asked, his eyes sweeping the room as if he were simply going to spot it for them.

Grace hadn't missed his inspection of the room. He'd come up behind at least five of the officers, seemingly peering over their shoulders at their tasks as they bagged and catalogued the room's contents.

Again that feeling of unease overcame her. Something about Heron Jane made her . . . nervous.

Was he the sort of inspector who sold information and photographs to the press? Maybe Arjun wasn't a prostitute at all, but an informant or—

Easy, Gray, her dead husband said. *Anyone ever tell you that you're paranoid?*

"Given the basilar and diastatic fractures and the surface area damaged by the impact, I would say he was struck twice. First like this"—Yin raised her hand and swung it left to right—"and then like this." She raised her hands over her head and brought them down. "The force delivered was considerable. The weapon, whatever it is, will have a round head on it."

Grace admitted that nothing matched that description as far as she could see.

It did, in fact, look like little more than a storage cabinet, with its shiny silver counters and little glass vials. Then there were the clear glass cabinets with supplies and unused equipment.

"If they were smart, they took the weapon with them," Heron said, obviously having missed their earlier conversation.

"Hide it or bury it," Grace agreed. "Only an idiot would leave it behind with their prints on it."

Yin scratched her nose with the back of her gloved hand. "I've scanned the skull and have a reconstruction running. In an hour or so, I should have a better sense of what happened and the definitive shape of the object we're looking for. Then I'll be knocking on Dr. Cyrah's door to ask her to identify it. My luck, it'll be something they have a *thousand* of."

"You just have to find the missing one," Heron said cheerfully.

Both Grace and Yin regarded him warily.

"A cakewalk," Yin said. She wasn't smiling.

"Good job," Grace told her.

Yin seemed to puff up at this praise. "Just doing what you taught me, Commander."

Grace knelt down and took a good hard look at Ravee's body. The way the arms stretched out as if reaching for something. His head turned, so that the right cheek was pressed to the floor. The blood circling the head like a saint's halo. The one eye they could see was open and milky white. His open mouth revealed a chipped front tooth and swollen tongue. With her eyes, she traced a blue vein from his temple down his arm to his hand. Blood pooled in the knuckles.

Fingers unmoving. Hands that would never touch Risa again.

A wave of gratitude struck Grace in the chest.

Nowhere in her memory did she have a grotesque image like this of her husband or son. She had only the moment of wide-eyed fear, and then the fire that consumed it. It had been quick, at least. She should be glad for that small mercy.

"Does she always get that close?" she heard Heron ask. "And, uh, *stare* like that?"

"Grace?" Yin said, and then as if remembering herself, she added, "Commander?"

"I'm all right," Grace said quietly.

And she was all right. She had no other choice but to look death directly in the eye.

SEVEN

TOGETHER IN THE CITYRIDE AUTO, heading back to the station, Grace thought it was best to deal with the situation now. Prolonging the inevitable for the sake of delicacy wouldn't make it easier.

"You photographed the scene and the body," Grace said. She stated it plainly instead of asking it as a question as Adams might have.

"Yes," Heron said. He had his chin on his hand, looking out the window at the passing traffic. A shadow fell across his face as a second-level transport passed overhead.

Grace tried not to fixate on the easy sprawl of his legs. The casual masculine posture he was adopting. In the corner of her eye, he looked too much like Davion.

"I've reconstructed the weapon, and I'm running it against Viscosity's inventory. Right now, I have six items that could've been used. I'm betting on the glass rod. Though the double-helix paperweight could have also done it."

"How could you have reconstructed the weapon already?" she asked, not bothering to hide her disbelief.

He tapped the side of his head. "I have all the software here."

"You don't have the clearance for that."

He only looked at her for a moment. He cocked his head. In that moment, he looked very much like a bird. "I thought it was my job to solve this."

"You're an assistant inspector. You interview suspects. You piece together data. You rely on a specialized team to gather the information you need, and then you process it. You do the legwork of whatever task *I* give you. You don't do whatever you want with information you don't have permission to have! You are part of a team."

"How has that worked out for you?" His voice dropped, flatlining. "Relying on a team?"

"What?" It was as if she'd been slapped. She felt the heat rise in her cheeks.

"Was there a team with you that night at the precinct? Or did you go into the building alone? Did you dismantle the bomb alone or did you form a team first and assign everyone wires and computer chips?"

Heat consumed her face. "How dare you."

He seemed to realize his error a heartbeat later. "Grace—"

"Stop the auto."

"Commander, *please*."

The CityRide pulled to the exit lane as instructed and began its exit speech.

"Thank you for using CityRide, your—"

Grace was out of the auto and marching down the sidewalk.

Heron was close on her heels.

"Commander, I'm sorry."

She said nothing. She couldn't have been more than nine or ten blocks from the precinct. She would walk there, and when she arrived, she would tell Adams that Jane wasn't working out. She didn't want him. She'd rather work alone than with—

Someone who speaks the truth? her dead husband asked.

"I'm sorry," Heron said, again overtaking her, then blocking her path.

"Move or I will move you."

"Okay," he acquiesced, though he kept close at her side. "But I didn't mean to imply that your family died because of something you did or didn't do."

She stopped, whirling on him. "Then what were you implying?"

She was struck by what she saw: grief. True grief engulfed his face. It was in the downward tilt of his eyes. The downward pull of his lips and the widening pupils.

She didn't need to run her lie-detection program to know he was sorry. But *this* sorry? It didn't add up.

"I shouldn't have said that. I don't know why I did. My mothers accuse me of speaking before I think."

"I'm not your mother, Jane. I'm not here to put up with your mouth or your personality quirks." Grace resumed marching toward the precinct. Two blocks, and then the pavilion and steps would appear before her. She side-stepped two little boys on their hoverskates and her heart lurched.

They looked nothing like Kaiden, but they didn't have to.

When will it stop? her heart begged to know. *When will the hurting* stop?

She was afraid she knew the answer.

"Can we please slow down for a moment? I want to speak to you before we get back to the precinct."

Before you're fired, you mean. Instead she said, "I don't care for how lax you are with protocol. You might have done things differently in your zone, but here we do things my way. And *my* way—"

"Saves people."

She saw red. "Are you *mocking* me?"

"No, no!" he was quick to say. "You did save people. You lost your family, but you saved thousands of lives."

He desperately searched her face for any sign of forgiveness. Finding none, he blundered ahead. "You asked me why I have the software. Let me tell you."

She didn't reply. She continued to use the pedestrian lane to cross. The precinct's circular drive came into view, and beyond that the hazy form of the precinct's public entrance.

"I have the software because I paid for it, but I suspect your real question is, why do I need it? I know you think I do things differently, but I can explain. I'll tell you the truth if you'll just *stop* and *listen* to me for two minutes."

"Two minutes. Go," she said, but she didn't stop walking.

"Maybe you don't have issues with corruption in your department, but in my old zone, we did. Many of the officers are owned by the corporations that can afford to pay them a retainer higher than their salaries. Evidence often disappeared. Witnesses, too. If I hoped to actually solve the cases that fell into my lap, I had to become a one-person team. Do you understand? I couldn't trust many of the other officers because I didn't know who owned whom."

She said nothing.

"I have every program, every tool I need to be my very own walking, talking crime-solving unit. There is no piece of evidence or interview that I can't conduct myself and store securely on my private server."

"That must cost a fortune," she muttered, her steps faltering. The math running in her head was staggering.

"My mother is very generous to her only child." He said it with absolutely no shame. "Have you really never bought personal upgrades?"

She had.

Grace stopped. She saw the precinct clearly now. One more intersection and they would be standing in the sunlit pavilion. She turned her back on the building.

She'd purchased the bomb program, hadn't she? Though it had been called unnecessary and outdated. She'd gotten the software just in case. And it hadn't been just bomb detection she'd invested in.

She turned on her lie-detection program.

"Why are you here? In this zone?" she asked.

"I want to help you," he said.

Truth.

"And can I trust you?"

Hurt flickered through his eyes. "I would never betray you, Grace."

Truth.

"Did you take this position to get away from the corruption in your old zone?"

He snorted, and it was a cold, angry sound. "I didn't want to come here. I think you've guessed as much by my initial attitude—"

Truth.

"—for which I am sorry," he added. "It isn't your fault. But the fact remains, I came, and I do intend to help you. However I can."

Truth.

"Interzone visas aren't so easy to come by."

He snorted again, placing hands on his hips. "You misunderstand how badly my old zone wanted to get rid of me."

Lie.

"No one likes having their corruption exposed and authority challenged."

Grace searched his face. So he wasn't telling the truth about where he came from or why he'd left. Maybe he didn't trust her with that information yet. After all, if he suspected the precinct of corruption, why would he? But he had promised not to betray her. Or at least he had no intentions to do so.

Fine. Everyone deserved to keep their own secrets. Heaven knew she had her own.

"Do you think our department is corrupt?" she asked him. "Do you think my husband and my son—"

"I don't know for sure what's going on here yet," he said. His voice was soft and sincere. "But I'm trying to work it out."

Truth.

Fire in her chest and face threatened to consume her. "If someone in my own department had a hand in their deaths—"

"We don't know that yet," he said.

Truth.

And it was the *we* that struck her. *We.* He was throwing his lot in with hers.

"I am sorry for the attitude earlier. I really am," he said again. "You'll get no more resistance from me."

"Clearly it wasn't your goal to be an assistant inspector," she said. "If you don't like the job—"

"Inspector isn't so bad under a worthy commander. I could get used to it." A weak smile played on his lips. "Maybe *I* will even be commander myself one day. Give me enough time to get everyone in the zone to fall in love with me."

His charming optimism was hard to ignore.

"Hoping to usurp me?" Grace asked as she resumed walking.

"No, I'll come for the other guy. He seems like the easier target."

Grace made a sound that could be mistaken for amusement.

"I'm sorry," he said one last time. "Grace, I really am."

"Apology accepted. Now let's go into my office, and you can catch me up on what your fancy software has told you about Ravee's murder."

He hesitated, running his hand up the back of his head. "Uh, Commander. Can I ask for one favor?"

But Grace barely heard him. She'd stumbled as her eyes fell on the rough shape of the figure in the center of the pavilion. At a distance, she had thought it was the Jolly Roger, a statue of the famed Commander Hank Roger, who had protected the city from a digital takeover in 2466.

But it wasn't his bronze-cast face staring down at her. It was hers.

Smooth and unblemished.

"I would appreciate it if you didn't mention to anyone that I have the upgrades. If you could—" Heron continued, oblivious to the tidal wave of emotion consuming her.

"No!" Grace yelled up into the face of the statue. "No! No! No!"

The sound of her escalating voice drew attention.

"Commander?"

"They can't do this! They can't!"

She couldn't let this happen. She just *couldn't*.

She would take it down. She would take it down by any means necessary. But she didn't have anything on her. She pulled her defense stick from her pocket, lengthened and doubled it until it was the size of her forearm, perhaps a bit larger. She expanded its large shield.

She struck the statue and a resounding metallic echo rang through the pavilion. She struck it again, this time across the perfect bronze of her face, scuffing it. If she kept it up, she could make it look scarred, a more accurate representation than this unblemished monstrosity.

"Whoa, whoa, whoa." Heron was on her before she managed to connect with the head of the statue for a sixth time.

"They can't!" she said. She knocked him off easily.

He pulled her down into a squat and spoke rapidly into her ear. "Gray, people will think you don't appreciate this, uh, honor if you take the shield to your face again."

Gray. God, he'd called her Gray. Only Davion had ever called her Gray.

Davion, Davion, Davion.

"They can't put a statue on the spot where my son and husband *died*. Don't they realize—d-don't they realize what they've done?"

"They want to honor your sacrifice."

"It wasn't a sacrifice. It was a failure. The biggest failure of my life."

Your heart rate is rising rapidly, Grace. Would you like to run the CALM program?

"No!" she shouted. "No, I would *not* like to run the fucking CALM program!"

Grace had the defense stick in her hands again, and instead of stopping her, Heron simply moved out of her way, giving her full access to the bronze statue.

She raised the electric shield high over her head.

"Commander," a voice called out.

Grace turned, shield wavering in her grip, and saw Commander Adams standing on the steps of the precinct.

Then she noticed that several others, mostly passersby

but some officers as well, lingered in the pavilion, on the sandstone steps, watching her.

"Can I speak to you?" Adams said calmly. "If you have a moment?"

Reluctantly, Grace lowered the shield. She tried to collapse it, but her hands shook.

"Give it to me," Heron murmured, and she handed it over without question.

She felt him slip it back into her pocket as they reached the precinct steps.

She tried not to look at anyone as she crossed the public section to the secured area. The three of them remained silent as they passed through the bio-seal and into the private section.

Grace heard the whir of the janitorial machine on the floor above as they passed into Adams's office.

He closed the door before speaking. She braced herself.

"What the hell, Grace?" he said. His tone was somewhere between surprised and annoyed. "Are you out of your mind?"

No more than usual, she thought.

"What in the world would make you take a defense stick to a statue in public? Are you *trying* to get suspended?"

She found her voice at last. "Take it down."

"It isn't even finished," he said. "It has at least two weeks of work left until it's done."

"I want it gone."

"Most officers would kill for some sort of acknowledgment. Why are you being like this?"

Grace gritted her teeth so hard her jaw hurt. "I want it *gone!*"

"As your co-commander, I have no jurisdiction over you, Buteo. But what I just saw in that pavilion raises serious concerns about your state of mind. I'm not sure—"

"You didn't tell her you were having a statue erected on the spot where her husband and son were *murdered*," Heron said pointedly. His voice hadn't risen. Nor had his eyes left Adams's. "How did you expect her to feel when she saw it? A permanent statue of her, standing over the spot where she lost everything. What were *you* thinking?"

Adams's gaze flicked between them. Reaching some conclusion, he exhaled. "I can see now that was rather insensitive."

"Worse than insensitive. It's disrespectful," Heron said.

Adams was searching Grace's face. "I'm sorry, Commander. It wasn't intended that way. We wanted to honor—"

"No, you wanted to remind me of what I've lost," she corrected. "Every day I walk into this building."

He frowned down at his hands. "I am not sure I can get the city commission to remove it. If I can, I will."

"Or have it boiled down and used for parts," Heron suggested. "Bronze is in high demand right now."

Adams wouldn't look at him. His eyes remained fixed on Grace's face. "Are you sure you're all right?"

The truth was, Grace *wasn't* sure. She felt as though a belt had been wrapped around her chest and someone was tightening it, pulling it harder and harder until she couldn't draw a full breath. What was getting through came in short, sharp pants.

"She was fine until she saw a twelve-foot statue of herself," Heron said. "We were discussing the Viscosity case, completely immersed in our work, and—"

"Grace—"

"I'm fine." She stood. She couldn't stay here. "But I want that statue gone."

Adams sighed, rubbing the top of his head. "I'll do my best."

Grace left the office without another word. She didn't owe Adams any more of an explanation than she'd already given him.

Heron caught up to her in the narrow hallway. "Where are we going?"

"My office. Our office," she amended.

She found the door and pushed it open with her hand. She found it how she'd left it.

And it was another blow to her heart.

On the wall were three drawings done by Kaiden. A red handprint made into a bird with the help of a few pen strokes, one of the earth, and a third of a satellite telling the moon a joke.

It hurt her to see this and yet it seemed so precious. Her mother had spared her the agony of packing away all their things and putting them in storage and reprogramming the house. Kaiden's room was empty now of painful reminders like this. Her mother had asked her if she wanted a home office but she'd declined, so now the second bedroom stood empty.

Heron followed her gaze. "Do you want me to take them down?"

"No," she said. How was looking at the picture any different than the thousands of self-tortures she'd inflicted every day since they'd died? "No. Leave them."

He turned then and saw her crestfallen expression. He shut the door behind them.

The moment the doors closed, her shoulders slumped.

"Do you need anything?" he asked. His voice was pitched low, as if he was worried the place was bugged.

"My mind."

"Is that it?" he asked with a half smile. "Good news. You still have it."

Do I? she wondered. *Do I really?*

She came around her desk and sat in the chair. Nothing had changed in her absence. She thought maybe someone had wiped it down, tidying it up for her, but she couldn't be sure. She'd kept it rather clean herself. But the picture of her and Davion sat on one corner of the desk. It was from South Africa, where they'd taken their honeymoon. Beside this photo were six or seven more pictures spanning their fifteen years together.

Heron was also staring at the photos. With tears in the corners of his eyes, he slid into the opposite chair. "How shall we proceed, Commander?"

"I don't know," she said. "But we have to."

Their calorie watches beeped again, in sync. "Food first and then back to the case?"

"It's getting late. We could call it a day. Do you have someone waiting at home?"

Heron shook his head. "No. I'm willing to burn the midnight oil if you want to keep working. We have plenty of data to process."

"Would you—I'm not trying to treat you like an errand boy, but —"

"Grace," he interrupted her. "It's okay. You can ask me for whatever you need."

The gentleness was too much. It hurt.

"I'd love a koffee. It helps me think." She knew the synthetic brand was too strong to drink this late in the day, but it was also a tenth of the price of natural coffee.

He jumped up and gave her an easy smile. "One koffee coming up. How do you take it?"

"A bullet and a half."

"Ooh," he said, gathering himself up and heading for the door. "You're tougher than you look."

If only that were true, she thought, and closed her eyes.

EIGHT

WITH A MOMENT TO HERSELF, Grace found composure. She pulled out her defense stick, a simple device that could conjure a repelling shield on command. She activated the shield now and ran her hand along its four sides, inspecting it for damage.

Maybe half her body would not be scarred, stiff, and unyielding had she thought to put this between herself and the exploding auto.

But she had only thought of reaching her husband and son as quickly as she could.

Had she been faster, perhaps she would be dead instead of disfigured. Had she found the second bomb as quickly as the first maybe they'd all be alive now.

She collapsed the shield with a sigh and slipped it back into her pocket.

Heron entered the office with a drink in each hand. Whistling a tune she didn't recognize, he handed the cup over her desk. "One black koffee for the commander."

She thanked him.

"Do you know that coffee—with a *c*—used to have two

main varieties? Arabica and Robusta. Robusta is the only natural bean that still exists today, but the koffee—with a *k* —that we drink is actually coffee with one genetic modification: it was spliced with the Kahnawake bean so it could survive our new climates. Hence *koffee*."

This was more information than Grace cared to know about her drink. What she wanted was the effect, no matter what it was called. But she was going to have to make adjustments and meet Heron somewhere in the middle.

"I have something for you," Grace said.

A smile, part amusement, part surprise, lit up his face when she opened the adjacent door and revealed the additional space. Undoubtedly it'd been mistaken for a closet, this long room with a large center table.

She was pleased to see this side office was still empty of all but the table, as if waiting for someone to fill it. It could have been taken over by anything during her leave of absence, to fulfill any of the thousands of needs the precinct had.

She imagined Duchovny or Adams fighting to keep this space *hers* despite her absence and the uncertainty whether or not she would make it in those first few days.

"This side will be yours," she said, gesturing toward the table. "I hope you don't mind that it's attached to mine. We will have to share a door, and we'll have to get you a chair."

"I'll steal the one from the commander's office."

"There are plenty of—"

"Yes, but I want *his*," he said with a devilish wink. "I'll put it back when I'm done."

"We can pull this table out and bring in whatever you—"

"Grace." He measured her again with that easy smile. "It's great. Really. It's more than I'd hoped for."

She watched him enter the room and put his koffee on the table, nodding as if agreeing with some unspoken statement.

She settled behind her own desk and opened her lenscape, reviewing the information she'd gathered throughout the day. She saw, vaguely, Heron leave the office and return, pushing a chair into his office.

She was aware that the precinct had grown dark and quiet, and that they were likely the only two bodies left in the building.

She reviewed the ninety-day cache that Adams had delivered as promised. It updated her on the status of funding requests and diplomatic affairs, as well as upcoming events and evaluations that needed attention. Then there were the officers' progress reports for nearly 250 open cases in the zone.

By the third koffee, her calorie watch beeped again.

"Do you like falafel?" he asked. And when she said she did, he fetched two from the mobile vender up the block.

"Now that you're settled in and I'm . . . *composed* . . . tell me what you took from the crime scene today," she said, accepting the warm pita with both hands. She was ready for the real work now that her mind was coming back to her. She felt calm enough to pay attention. Finally.

He settled into the chair opposite her desk.

<<Accept private chat with heronjane1?>>

His fingers tapped furiously at the tabletop and disappeared when her own screen was overtaken by the chat screen. "Let's start with the images," he said aloud.

One after another, Grace opened and reviewed the different photos.

He paused long enough to take a bite of his falafel wrap. Grace, unconsciously, did the same.

"I'm fairly certain the murder weapon was a glass rod." Heron pulled one of the photos to the center frame. "I've run the complete inventory of the building against my Imprint program, and it's the only item that matches the fractures in the back of Ravee's head. I wanted to know how many they actually have on the premises and if any are missing. I was only able to answer the first question. Over fourteen hundred are listed in their inventory. I can't even figure out what they use them for."

"It's unlikely that they've kept track of every glass rod in the building."

He sighed. "Right. But there are finder programs that I like to use. They're designed for kids, actually."

Grace's chest tightened. "I know."

The falafel faltered on its way to Heron's mouth.

She pressed on as if she hadn't noticed. "Kaiden had one. I gave it to him for his last birthday. He was always losing things."

Why did I bring him up? Grace thought. *Here come the apologies. Another wave of unbearable sympathy that will surely drag me under.*

But Heron surprised her. "I think if I use a program like that, I could find the weapon."

"How can you pick it out of a lineup of fourteen hundred glass rods?"

"Good question." He chewed on his lower lip, giving himself over to thought. "It could have a defect from the blows or residue. But if the murderer was intelligent, they'd wash it at least."

Something in Grace relaxed. *Maybe he wasn't the sort to pry. To offer condolences for the sake of making himself feel better.*

It wasn't that she minded being removed from the

equation of her grief. She preferred it. But dealing with the emotional burden of others' feelings was more than she could handle now. Their guilt. Their underlying tremor of fear and secret relief that because tragedy had struck so close, they were now immune, statistically speaking. They would be able to kiss their children goodnight. Curl into bed with their partners. All because the universe had rolled the dice and had taken its tithe from her. They'd been spared. And the only way to enjoy that pardon was to lay their sympathy at her feet.

Heron was still speaking, still flashing photos in front of her eyes as his fingers drummed on the tabletop. "Once I have the rod, I could run BlackLite for prints and evidence."

"Remember, we aren't trying to solve the murder of Ravee Kapur. We are trying to find the missing organs."

"Ouch," Heron said with mock offense. "Don't you have faith in my ability to multitask?"

She took another bite of falafel. "I think it's the same case."

"Me too."

"Which is why I just officially opened it as a subcase and named us lead investigators, at least until the initial groundwork is laid. But we can't forget the real reason we were called to Viscosity."

"Uh-huh," he said. And it was so like Davion she had to stop herself from saying, *Are you listening to me?*

She swallowed. "I'll focus on finding the organs, and you focus on finding the killer, and see if we don't meet somewhere in the middle?"

"Perfect. Where will you start?"

She terminated their shared chat, downloading his remaining crime scene data as a cache, and reclaimed her lenscape.

"I'm running all the footage from the building surveillance now."

On the left side of her lenscape, she let the footage of Viscosity's two entrances flow. Every time a face appeared, she pulled it from the footage and matched it to the Identit-E program running in the middle of her lenscape. On the right, a list of names of everyone who entered and exited the building was being processed. If she couldn't match a name to a face, she would pull it for her follow-up list.

Another passing face caught Grace's eye, and she turned away from Heron. Transfixed by the ghostly visage, she cried out.

"What?" he asked, pausing midbite.

"It's Lake," she said. "He walked through Viscosity's employee entrance at"—she located the time stamp—"23:53."

She pinged Heron and offered to share her lenscape with him. He accepted, sitting up in anticipation.

The footage rolled of Lake passing the employee bioscreener and entering the stairwell adjacent the entrance.

Grace skipped to the two-minute mark and waited for Lake to appear. The stairwell door opened, and there he was, mouth open in deep breaths—surely from ascending nine flights quickly—a bag slung over his shoulder. He entered the lab.

No camera footage could be found for the three minutes he was inside. But then Grace saw the problem.

Exiting the restroom and heading down the long hall toward the lab was Ravee Kapur. He pushed his dark hair back from his face.

Grace waited for Lake to exit the lab and the conflict to ensue.

"But he dies in another lab," Heron murmured as if reading her mind.

"Shhh," she said, hoping the silence would hold. She wanted to take in every detail of these crucial moments. She saw the wrinkles in Kapur's protective lab coat. She saw his hand dragging under his nose. She saw the tense exhaustion causing his shoulders to droop.

The lab door opened, and she sucked in a breath.

Lake stepped out of the lab into the hallway, a large sack over one shoulder. A sack presumably full of organs. *Eight kidneys, six livers, four hearts, three pancreases, three lungs, a thymus, and even a pair of eyes.*

Morbidly, Grace wondered where the eyes might be. On the top or bottom of the bag? Surely the top, or they'd be squished.

"How do you think he stuffed them in there? Did he wrap them up or—"

"*Shhhhh*," Grace insisted.

"There's no audio on this tape," Heron said, the pout in his voice unmistakable. "It's not like I'm talking over them."

"I can't listen to you and pay attention at the same time."

She rewound the last thirty seconds and started again. The lab door opened and Lake stepped into the hallway with his sack.

And there was Kapur.

And nothing.

No fight.

No yelling, no surprise.

The men stopped in the hall and exchanged words. Lake looked confident. A big smile. Direct eye contact. Casual gesticulations punctuating his words. But gently, not in threat or anger.

Ravee was also at ease. His smile was a little more restrained in something like remorse, if Grace had to guess. And then the men parted. Ravee went back into the lab.

That was when Lake's cool demeanor changed.

The moment Ravee turned his back on Lake and reentered the lab, Lake broke into a run. He flew down the hallway with his organ sack bouncing heavily against those straining shoulders. The easygoing look Lake had worn just a moment before was dramatically replaced by urgent desperation.

Ah, Grace thought. *So the show is over.*

Lake was out of sight and down the corridor before the lab door was fully shut. He was in the stairwell, presumably rushing down nine flights of stairs toward the exit—which a later camera check would confirm. He'd reached the third floor landing by the time the lab door opened again and revealed an also-changed Ravee.

Instead of panic and urgency, Grace saw fury and outrage on Ravee's face.

"What did I just see?" Heron said, falling back into his seat. "Did Lake kill him?"

As if Grace had said anything.

"He can't have. Lake ran toward the stairs. The lab where we found him is in the opposite direction."

Grace wasn't listening. She was fixated on Ravee's expression when he saw Lake in the hallway.

"Ravee wasn't surprised to see him," Grace said, replaying the scene again up until the moment when Ravee burst from the lab. "Only when he goes back into the lab and sees the organs are missing does he even get upset."

"Can someone enter a bio-sealed building if they aren't coded for it?"

"No."

"Maybe Lake's a hacker," Heron said.

"A hacker who shows up in company pictures," Grace said. "We're *really* going to have to interview Dr. Cyrah again."

"The receptionist said she wasn't free until Thursday."

Grace ignored this. "Lake *must* have been an employee there. We'll ask her about the people in the photo."

"Wait," Heron said. "This means Lake is in this zone even though he doesn't exist in the network."

Her heart pounded.

"Have you ever heard of anything like this?" he asked.

Yes, she thought. And she saw the face of the man imprisoned for implanting two IEDs at the Zone 2 precinct.

Lix Richards.

A ghost who wasn't supposed to exist. No record. No past.

And yet he'd been real enough to reach out his hand and take everything she loved in an instant. The courts concluded that he'd erased all traces of himself because he wanted to destroy their security from the inside.

That he was a radical who'd somehow slipped through their thorough immigration process.

She forced herself to speak. "You can't move around a zone off-network. You can't buy food or housing or enter private buildings. It would be an impossibly hard life. Undoubtedly you'd be found and exiled."

"And yet here's a man who doesn't exist, entering a bio-sealed building," Heron whispered in awe. " Do you think he deleted himself?"

Run the CALM program?

For fuck's sake. No, she thought.

She stared at the back of her hands in her lap. At the

creases over each of her knuckles. She contemplated how one arm contained bone, another circuitry. Her past and her present. The world had remade her as it saw fit. Didn't it always?

"How do you trace the invisible?" she asked herself.

"Is muttering to yourself a commander habit or should I be concerned?"

"A spyder." Grace terminated the connection between them, revealing Heron's face. She looked away. "A spyder," she said again, tapping the tabletop.

"A spider?" Heron took the last bite of his falafel and crumpled the wrapper in his hand before looking around the room for the bin. "You know, they're very industrious. They were here before the dinosaurs. And if they decided they wanted to eat us, they could clean us right off the face of the planet in a couple of years. They far outnumber us."

"Spyder with a *y*," Grace said. "I'll take the biometric readings from Lake's entry into Viscosity, as well as the captures of his face, and I'll put a few spyders in the network. They'll check the entire zone for his readings and face. It's probably the only way we can find someone in the system who isn't listed. But if he's ever walked in front of a camera…"

Her voice trailed off as she realized this plan wasn't foolproof. They'd grabbed Lix right off the street. He'd been spotted running from the pavilion with everyone else, but he'd been the only unregistered face in sight.

She didn't want to think of Lix Richards's face the last time she saw him, sitting in the transparent cell at the jailhouse, claiming that he was innocent of the deaths of her husband and son. That he didn't create the explosive that took their lives, almost took her own, and injured nearly thirty-two people.

I didn't do this, he'd insisted, looking her in the eye with such sincerity she'd believed him.

How stupid. Worse, she hadn't even considered running her Truth program on him. She should have. What else would a criminal facing exile to the stormlands say?

Yet here was another ghost come to haunt her.

"Heron," Grace said carefully. It was time to find out if he was as trustworthy as she hoped. "I need you to know something."

He arched both brows and steepled his fingers. "Might I suggest a private chat over a secure line on my personal server then?"

"Yes." Her heart skipped a beat. Why was he so prepared for a cloak-and-dagger conversation?

<<Accept private chat with MrBlue?>>

She noted the name change.

<<Is there another bomb in the building?>> he asked.

<<No.>> Her thoughts about Richards stuttered in her mind. <<Wait. Why would I know if there was another bomb?>>

<<You identified the last one, didn't you?>>

<<Yes.>>

<<And how, might I ask, did you accomplish that?>>

Her heart began to pound again. <<You're not the only one with upgrades.>>

Then, << How did you know I was the one who'd spotted the IED first? You've been reading up on me.>>

<<I don't deny it,>> he said with a casual grin. <<I wanted to know more about you before I agreed to work for you.>>

<<Don't believe everything you read.>> Her fingers fumbled with the edge of the falafel wrapper. It was brown with the restaurant logo stamped onto its corner.

She tried not to, but she already saw the wide whites of Kaiden's eyes as he pressed his small hands to the auto's window. His palm flattened on the glass. His mouth open in a silent *Mom!*

The glimpse of Davion's arm as he flung it over the boy's shoulder, pulling him back into his protective embrace.

Then the fire. The explosion. The vertical lift.

<<Grace?>>Heron asked gently. <<What do you want me to know?>>

<<The only other man I've known to travel the zone off-network is Lix Richards.>>

Heron didn't seem to understand the significance.

<<He's the man accused of setting off the IED. He's the one who killed my husband and son.>>

Heron blinked. <<Oh.>>

<<If Adams knows I'm working a case with another off-network suspect, they'll say he's also a terrorist. That they must belong to the same network and I... >> She wasn't sure how to finish the text. The blinker hovered in her vision. She sent it without completing it.

<<He will have you removed from the case, which is ridiculous because objectivity is futile. No one is objective.>>

<<I wanted you to know so that we could keep this detail to ourselves. For now.>>

<<Okay.>>

And at that, Grace thought the line had been terminated. But then Heron sent another message along the wire. <<Do *you* think there's a connection between Richards and Lake?>>

"Maybe," she said aloud, even as her heart said *yes*.

NINE

GRACE KNEW that the time for sleep had come. She couldn't pursue Lake until she had a trail, and she had to wait for the spyder to create one. She and Heron agreed to go their separate ways at midnight.

Heron walked with her to the CityRide stop but, after a polite goodbye, headed east. He walked with his head bent in thought, hands in his pockets, in the opposite direction of his home.

Maybe he didn't sleep.

Maybe he was meeting up with Arjun—or someone else.

None of it is my business, she reminded herself on the quiet CityRide to her house.

Davion had been her business. And Kaiden. Now that business was over.

Now there was only her.

"Welcome home, Grace," the house said as the garage opened and the lights flickered on.

She stepped into the kitchen to find an ensaymada on

the countertop. Sugar gleamed along its surface as well as the countertop.

"I should recalibrate your arms," she told the silent ChefMate. It was obvious from the circle of granulated sugar that it had missed its mark. And sugar was not cheap. She could only guess what else her mother might have ordered for her. She was too tired to look in the fridge and see.

"Grace, you have one message. Would you like to hear it?" the house said.

"Okay," she said before forking a bite of the buttered brioche. The sugar and cheese scraped across the roof of her mouth.

She wondered if this was her mother's plan for dealing with her grief—drowning her in food.

"Gracie, it's me. Do you like the ensaymada I ordered? If not, unload it on your coworkers, but I think it's amazing. I also got you something else. I *really* hope you like him."

Him?

Grace paused, her fourth bite hovering on its way to her mouth. A dawning horror grew in her consciousness. She groaned. "*No.*"

"I put it in the hall closet since there was room."

"Oh *no.* Mom, you didn't," she said aloud, though the older woman was likely asleep in her own bed eight miles away. Grace set the fork down and crossed from the kitchen to the living room.

Down the adjacent hallway, she stopped in front of the closet. She took a breath and opened the door. Her fears were confirmed.

"Dammit, Mom."

"If you don't like him, we can always send him back,"

the message went on. "But just give it a few days. He might grow on you."

Grace pressed her fingers into her temples. "*Mom.*"

There was no point in arguing with a prerecorded message. But she would've if it meant this six-foot Boi would magically disappear from her closet.

Its very presence disturbed her. As if sleep wasn't going to be hard enough to find tonight with Lix Richards weighing on her mind and the vast emptiness of her bed.

Now she was going to have to forget that there was a *naked* Boi in her downstairs closet, waiting for her to wake it up and give it a purpose.

She surveyed the delicate closed eyelids, the dark hair falling across the face.

It reminded her of Heron, actually, if he had a wider face, more slant to his eyes, and longer hair. She touched the skin, and it was warm.

Too much like real skin. It felt like flesh and bone beneath.

As real as my right arm, anyway.

She shut the closet door.

Then she opened it again, searching for an auto-start setting. The last thing she needed was to wake up with it standing over her in the night. She found the Boi set to *off* and closed the door again.

Muttering angrily, she climbed the stairs to her dark bedroom. She stripped down to nothing and stepped into the adjacent bathroom.

She pulled her ToothBlast from the counter and inserted it into her mouth. Waited for the blue light flash and then set it down on the glass shelf before climbing into the shower.

Alerted to her presence, the water turned on. She disabled the auto wash, preferring to run her hands through her own hair tonight. She hoped the motions would ease some of the tension between her shoulder blades. The shower would help her sleep.

You have one unplayed Informed Citizen report, her lenscape announced.

Before she could stop it, the program began.

It was mandatory, of course, that every citizen hear the bulletin produced for the previous twenty-four hours. She'd simply run out of delay prompts and couldn't postpone it any longer.

She sighed and tilted her head back into the hot water.

"National News: Water shortages continue to persist in Zones 99, 131, 144, 168, 209, and 311. Citizens may revert or donate their water to affected areas. Solar activity remains consistent and energy production is at maximum capacity for most zones. However, solar grids 1163 and 1275 are down for maintenance following a storm surge. Zones 208 through 213 will be without power until maintenance is complete."

Well, that's what you get for living too close to the stormlands, she thought.

They don't have a choice, Gray.

Her hands faltered in her hair at the sound of Davion's voice. Yes, that would be tonight's memory, she decided. The one she would fall asleep to.

She exited the shower, dressed for bed, and slid between her sheets. Then she rolled on her side, facing Davion's empty pillow. She ran a hand over the cool fabric.

Grace relaxed into the pillow. "Memory bank."

Her lenscape awoke again, offering her a list of all recorded memories.

Grace saw the one she wanted, recognizing it by its thumbnail cover. "Play memory twelve forty-two."

A pause and then Davion appeared beside her, lying on his side, facing her. "What's wrong?" he asked.

Grace didn't speak, choosing instead to listen to all of her old fears secondhand.

"I don't think I can do this," she told him.

"It's recognition you deserve," he assured her. He reached across the bed and pulled her close. She saw all this, but she felt nothing. The sheets in her bedroom didn't move, nor her position on her pillow. Her dead husband was talking to another wife. A wife without a scarred face and lost arm. A wife whose husband and son had not died. "You *deserve* to be recognized for all that you've done for this zone."

"But there's so much more I should be doing. What if I let them down?"

"You could never," he said and laughed. "You're amazing and the job hasn't changed, just what they call you."

"Maybe they shouldn't. Maybe Maverick should be Commander."

Davion laughed. "Maverick voted for *you*."

"Just because people choose something doesn't mean it's the right choice."

He frowned, cupping her cheek.

In that moment, it was as if he were alive again. He was stretched long beside her. His eyes were searching her own.

Be alive, she wished. *I'd give anything if you were just alive.*

"You have to celebrate this victory, Gray. If you can't celebrate this, you'll never be able to appreciate how lucky we are."

And maybe she didn't appreciate it.

Davion had transferred in from one of the furthermost zones. He'd earned that privilege with his indispensable network skills and landed a job at the top programming firm, Charlotte's, securing his visa straight out of university.

He didn't talk about his home zone much. They'd never returned to visit, as Davion had no surviving family, so Grace hadn't seen the place with her own eyes. She'd asked once if he wanted to take Kaiden back so that he could see where Davion grew up and went to school.

Maybe. When he's old enough to understand.

She suspected the real reason was that he hadn't wanted to go back. There was a melancholy in his eyes she hadn't understood when he spoke of *home*.

Maybe he hadn't believed Grace would understand either. She'd been born in Zone 2, went to university in Zone 4, and moved back when she got a good job. These were the wealthiest zones in the country. Perhaps she didn't have Heron Jane's money to throw around on the latest gadgets or processing-speed boosts, but what did she know about scarcity? About high waters or storms so terrible that one wayward wave decimated a community for years?

Just because her ancestors had been the first to move further inland, to buy up all the centermost land in the country in order to escape the rising waters, it didn't mean she deserved to be here.

They'd done the hard work, the stringent, economical use of land and water. *They'd* designed and implemented the city filters to control the methane and CO_2 in the air. *They'd* invested in the purification technology and industrious levees that kept the water clean and regulated.

Resource management was law. It was how they survived.

"We are so lucky," he said as if on cue.

Maybe we were, but not anymore.

"It's difficult to feel like this isn't a mistake," her long-ago self said.

"I know. But within a year, you'll wonder why you ever looked back." His bright smile broke her heart. "It's what I love about you. You're always looking around the next corner. If something does creep up on us, you'll be the first one to see it. You'll keep us safe."

She reached out to touch her husband's smiling face, finding only smooth, cool bamboo fabric as the memory clicked off, leaving her in a silent bedroom.

"If only that had been true, Davion," she said to the encroaching darkness. *If* only *that had been true.*

TEN

"GRACE," the house said. "You have a visitor at the door."

Grace removed the ToothBlast from her mouth and put it on the glass shelf beneath the mirror. At the top of the stairs, she called out, "Show me."

The house obliged by removing the opacity on the front wall. What was solid a moment before became as transparent as glass.

Heron stood on the step at the front door, head bent, the walkway stretching out behind him.

"Wall up. And please let Inspector Jane inside."

She descended the stairs.

"Welcome, Inspector Jane. We're so happy to see you," the house said, adding his name and biosignature to the household memory.

Heron crossed the threshold, smiling. "I come bearing gifts."

He offered her the koffee, her customary black.

"How did you know where I live?" she asked. She met him in the living room, reaching out to accept the offering.

She'd been about ten minutes from leaving for the office. It was more than a little strange that he should find her here.

"It's listed in the department registry," he said. His chipper demeanor faltered. "And honestly, if you believe that IED was intended for you, that should be struck from the record."

He had a point. And missed another.

"My worst fear has already come to pass. I'm not worried about another bomb."

He simply stared at her. "Torture, then? Bodily harm?" He seemed to catch himself. "*More* bodily harm?"

Her jaw clenched. "Showing their face would be the last thing they ever do."

Heron looked ready to say more but didn't. Instead, he let his gaze slide away, over the living room with its high ceiling, the opacity set at zero. Grace liked it that way, with nothing but a bright sky above her. In the kitchen, the ChefMate was cleaning up the egg and toast breakfast it had made for her.

When Grace had inspected the menu, she saw that her mother had programmed over fifty meals in the next two weeks—including nine desserts. She'd finally gotten around to pausing it to give her time to finish the leftovers.

"Your home is lovely. Two bedrooms?"

"Yes," she said. "Though I suppose I should downsize."

"I doubt they'll enforce that as long as your consumption remains in range for one person. You're working so much, I can't imagine you'd ever go above your allotment."

"I love watching futbol," she said. "That takes quite a bit of energy."

"Futbol?" He smiled. "Well, definitely a studio for you then."

"Why did you meet me here?" she asked, pulling a piece of the ensaymada from a plate on the counter and stuffing it into her mouth. It went well with the koffee. She offered it to Heron, who took a generous piece for himself.

"I wanted to make sure you didn't go to Kapur's alone," he said before filling his own mouth. "You have it listed at the top of the case file, so I thought it was your first task of the day. Was I wrong?"

He wasn't. She wanted to get that out of the way first and knew that telling the fiancée of her loss was undoubtedly going to be an unpleasant job.

"No," Grace admitted. "We need to interview her again."

"Good Grackle, *that* is delicious. What is that? Is that *cheese*? *And* sugar?"

"Ensaymada. It's Filipino. My mother ordered it. It seems she's hijacked my ChefMate."

"I don't know what you're complaining about. It's amazing."

"Yes, well, my mother isn't paying the household account," she said.

"Brioche! *Yes*. That's it," he said as if just realizing something. He reached toward the plate again. "May I?"

"We can bring it if you want."

"I want. But can I use your restroom before we catch an auto?"

"Around the corner. On the right."

She crossed to the wall to adjust the conservation status before she left. No need to run more than the household's bare essentials while she was away. But the panel was blinking red.

Update mode, please try again later.

Strange. She couldn't remember the last time the house had been in update mode.

"Last night I was thinking," Grace began, throwing her voice over her shoulder, hoping Heron could hear her. "We should try to access Ravee's memory bank. He might have stored his memories on a personal server. A lot of people do, myself included. We can get permission from the fiancée when we visit her. We'll likely need a permit from the constable, but given the circumstances—"

Heron grumbled something.

She came around the corner and found him standing in front of the hall closet. The naked Boi stood erect in the dark.

"The *other* right-side door," she said, feeling the heat rise in her face.

Heron put a hand on his hip. "It sort of looks like me."

"My mother picked it out," Grace said defensively. "I had nothing to do with how it looks."

"When did she give it to you?"

"Yesterday."

Heron wouldn't look away from him. "Your mother sounds . . . fascinating. All my mother ever gives me are books, and if I'm good, very thick socks."

"What about all your fancy gadgets?"

"Oh, yes, and money too," he amended.

She shifted uncomfortably. "Could you please—"

"Yes, sorry." He shut the door. "One second."

Grace had a chance to compose herself before Heron stepped out of the bathroom.

"I think the memory bank is a good idea," Heron said, grabbing his koffee from the counter and following her to the door with the ensaymada plate in his other hand.

"Thank you for visiting, Inspector Jane. Have a good day, Grace," the house said as she closed the door and waited for the sound of the auto-lock.

"Do you think Bois have memory banks?" Heron said as they followed the walkway. "Wouldn't those be fun to watch?"

· · ·

As Grace expected, the follow-up interview with Risa was even worse than the first. As soon as Risa opened the door and saw their faces, she devolved into sobs and collapsed into Grace's arms.

It was the same with me, Grace thought.

When Commander Adams had appeared in the hospital doorway, his hat in his hands, she'd known it was really true. Her eyes hadn't deceived her. Any lingering hopes that her husband and son had somehow survived had vanished.

"I'm sorry," Adams had said, shoulders hunched, his eyes red-rimmed.

"I'm sorry," she said to Risa now.

Heron entered Risa's kitchen and helped himself to the electric kettle. She wanted to tell him to stop, to sit down and act like an inspector. But his back was to her, so Grace was forced to endure the sound of the cabinets opening and closing and Risa's deep, desperate sobs.

Heron busied himself with making tea while the ensaymada sat in the middle of Risa's dining table. It looked wrong there. They shouldn't have brought it.

"I know this is hard for you," Grace said. "But I have to ask a few more questions."

Risa's sobs made Grace's chest hurt. She didn't want to say anything that would escalate or antagonize Risa, but she had an objective.

Heron finally found a mug.

"Is there anyone who would've wanted to hurt Ravee? Anyone with a grudge or unsettled—"

"No. Absolutely not. I mean, he could be an asshole when he played cards with his friends. Gloating, you know.

He was terrible when he won. But he always gave the money back. He was a kind man. The *kindest* man."

Grace wondered if this was how everyone else felt around her when confronted with her grief. Were they paralyzed, unsure of what to say? Did they labor over the choice: was it better to be silent or offer sympathy? To touch or not to touch?

"I can't believe this is happening. I just can't believe it." Risa sniffed into her cupped hands. "How am I supposed to go on? How am I? *How?*"

She looked at Grace as if she had the answers. Grace said nothing. What could she say? *Play him beside you at night. Play the memories you need to replay. Pretend that he's still alive, still living and breathing beside you. Conjure his face and voice whenever you want him. It will hurt. But it'll hurt less than the emptiness chewing you apart from the inside.*

Risa slid into the chair. "I'm sorry. My god, *Ravee.*"

It was unclear if she was apologizing to them or apologizing to her dead fiancé.

"You can still help us tremendously," Grace said, hoping to end the repetitious apologies and settle the business at hand. "If we could have your permission, we'd like to access Ravee's memory bank. We aren't looking for anything intimate or private. We only want the last few hours of his life. Anything that might help us piece together what happened."

Grace wanted to make sure it was clear what they were looking for in his memory bank. Some partners refused on the simple grounds they didn't want police reviewing footage where they might be seen naked or engaging in sex.

"I consent," she said before blowing her nose into the tissue. A desperate honking sound that Heron's mother would likely attribute to a goose.

Grace clipped that five-second sound bite and sent it to the constable. The green checkmark flashed and then was gone.

She could've terminated the recording then, having gotten what they needed for the record-keeping portion of her job, but Grace let the taping continue. Not because she wanted to document Risa's suffering, but because she found it easier, when these incidents went to trial, to be able to present interviews intact and unaltered. It improved jury perception of police reliability by nearly 83 percent.

"I must inform you that I am taping this conversation," Grace said kindly.

Risa nodded.

"I want to know who hurt him," Risa said, her wet eyes shining. "I want them thrown on the Midnight Train. I want them to starve in the stormlands!"

Risa looked up to find Heron placing a cup of tea on the table in front of her and pressing a tissue into her hand.

"So do we," Heron said sympathetically. "So do we."

ELEVEN

IT WASN'T until they were standing on the street outside the unit that Grace asked him about it. "Why do you do that?"

Heron looked up. "Do what?"

"Give women drinks," she said. She felt her irritation rising. It was nonsensical. She knew her irritability stemmed from her lack of sleep the night before. After she played not one but three memories of Davion on a loop for nearly six hours, she'd found herself no closer to getting the rest she needed. Perhaps it had been the nap she'd taken in the afternoon or the sugar she had too close to bedtime.

Or the grief consuming you, she thought.

"My mother taught me that," Heron said.

"The ornithologist?"

"No, the professor. Whenever I was upset, or if I was studying or puzzling over my castles, she would bring me a hot drink. She said the smallest gestures can help the most. It's become automatic when I see someone upset. I don't think about it anymore."

"Oh." She wasn't sure what else to say. "That's a great habit."

"Not just women though."

"What?"

"It's not just for women," he said with a smile. He was studying her face again with curiosity. "I bring men drinks too."

She couldn't repress a small smile.

"Was there something Davion used to do for you?" he asked. "A small, soothing gesture to punctuate a difficult day?"

There were a hundred actions Davion took that made the knots in her back and stomach loosen. A kiss at the temple or on the nape of her neck while they were in bed. His arms sliding around her waist as he stepped up behind her. Always opening the door to let her into the house, before the programming could do it.

"We would sit together on the sofa at night, after work and I'd tell him about the cases I was working on. While I worked it out, considered my next moves, he would pull my feet into his lap," she said.

Hearing the words leave her mouth was like an out-of-body experience. She was watching herself tell Heron this intimate story, unsure why she was doing it, yet unable to stop herself.

"He would rub them, first one then the other. He never interrupted me. He only listened. By the time I was done talking, I usually knew what I needed to do."

Heron was regarding her with an expression she didn't recognize. But before she could access her emotion scanner, he looked away, up the sidewalk.

When he turned back, his eyes were down, reading something on his lenscape. "The approval for the memory bank came through."

"Oh, good," she said, feeling more than a little put off that she'd just shared something so personal and it hadn't merited the smallest response from him.

If Heron noticed her discomfort, he didn't show it. For the first time in their two days together, he was starting to act like a professional. "Ravee Kapur used a server hosted by Felicity Designs. Their office is in Eastside. They've offered to show it to us whenever we come by."

"Then let's go," she said and put in the request for an auto.

FELICITY DESIGNS WAS A SQUAT BUILDING BETWEEN A corner grocery and the library, just north of Eastside Medical Clinic.

Because the building was little more than a glorified storage unit, the foot traffic outside was thin. Passersby were more interested in replenishing their pantries from the corner market or grabbing the latest copy of Koda Jones's book, *In Her Darkest Dreams*, advertised on the flashing digital bulletin on the front of the library.

"Do you like her?" Grace asked on impulse, motioning toward the flashing banner.

"Jones? Oh yes. She's amazing. It only takes her *one* day to produce a ninety-thousand-word masterpiece."

"She's a robot. She doesn't eat or sleep."

"She does have that advantage. Of course it takes her editors a few days to ready the book for publication. She has a whole team, and they have to recalibrate her after every novel, or so I hear. But her stories are so surprising."

"If you like bizarre hyperrealism. I suppose it's her material. She can't very well draw from experience, can she?"

Heron laughed. "What a snob you are, Commander. I

suppose you also dislike Polyphonic Phil on the same principle?"

Grace recognized the name of the robot musician. "Actually I think he's very good."

"Wouldn't you agree that music comes from the soul too? And from experience? If you can appreciate its expression in one art form, why not the other?"

When Davion would try to bait her with such arguments on art or philosophy, she would always give him a look that stopped him in his tracks. He'd laugh then. *Sorry. I'm not trying to change your mind. It's just force of habit. My old alma mater insisted we take up these arguments whenever they presented themselves. It was all in the name of critical thinking.*

He hadn't talked about his university days much, and now Grace deeply regretted not asking. She should have recorded his every thought. His every idea. Every memory and dream. If only she'd known that one day that was all she'd have left of him.

"Too early in the day for a debate?" Heron asked with a good-natured smile and let his curiosity die. He motioned toward the building. "Not much to look at, is it?"

Felicity Designs was bio-sealed. As they stepped up to the door, the AI requested they stand on the foot markers and accept the bio-scan procedure that would read their embedded ID and city registration. They obliged.

"Approved. Thank you for visiting Felicity Designs. Satisfaction guaranteed."

Heron snorted.

"What?" Grace crossed the threshold to find herself in a small receiving area. It didn't have the double-opt-in screen procedure that the precinct and even Viscosity had indulged in. Of course, not all companies could afford it.

"Their slogan *satisfaction guaranteed*. I can't tell if that's an excellent example of bravado or lazy copywriting." He rubbed his nose and sniffed. "Do you know that bio-scanners didn't take hold until the late twenty-four hundreds? The earliest forms of bio-reading were done by a microchip the size of a rice grain embedded in the hand. Between thumb and forefinger."

"Why'd they stop?"

"Human traffickers were cutting the chips out of the people they kidnapped to avoid detection. Then they were kidnapping citizens and reimplanting the chips in themselves to sneak into the protected zones. That's what it took to finally tackle human trafficking. Our mystery ghosts aside, this is an improvement, but it took two hundred years to manufacture and get zonewide bio-screening into the mainstream."

"Couldn't someone bring in a corpse?"

He smiled. "I admire your morbidity, but no. Not even if they cart around your dead body. Today's bio-scans check for a beating heart. You can thank William Tandy for that. He tried to rob a bank in 2508 with his taxidermized wife in tow. She was the bank manager. He just set her up in the lobby, hoping—"

Whatever he intended to say next was swallowed up by the thunderous steps of a very short woman marching toward them. Her short, quick strides added a tense urgency to the moment.

"Commander Buteo, Inspector Jane. Welcome to Felicity Designs. I'm Yuka Dane. If you'll follow me, I'll take you to a private screening room."

Obediently, they followed the short woman with the staccato steps through the small receiving area down a narrow passageway to a door at the end.

As the door opened, the ceiling dimmed its opacity. Sunlight poured in from overhead.

Both Heron and Grace looked up at the same time.

"Sorry," Yuka said with an apologetic grin. "The cloudy day has us running on reserve. We're trying to refill the chargers."

"Do you know that Elenora Karlsson invented the one-way glass we use in our solar sensors?" Heron said, admiring the transparent ceiling above. "The whole idea of full-building sensors was one budget cut away from being trashed altogether. People were outraged by the idea that satellites could see into their homes in the name of energy conservation. But when she figured out how to temper the glass so light can pass but not imaging technology, she saved the industry."

Yuka smiled politely, clearly unimpressed. "Here is the screening room."

"It's like you people don't *enjoy* learning," Heron muttered under his breath.

Yuka closed the door behind them and pointed to the cluster of chairs in the center of the room. "You'll find the tables in the side pockets of the chairs."

They did, pulling them up from between the cushions and arms and folding them over their laps.

"You both have the P^2 implant, I hope?" she asked.

"Yes," Heron said.

"I have the S^7," Grace said. "Does that matter?"

"No," Yuka said, giving her attention to something in the lenscape. "This will link as far back as the S^4."

"If it doesn't, I'll scapeshare," Heron said, leaning back into his chair with the casual air of a sultan on his throne.

"All right, here we go," Yuka said. "Place your proxies on the table."

They did as they were instructed.

The tables lit blue immediately, scanning the pinky side of their hands pressed onto the table.

"I've given you temporary access to Ravee Kapur's stream."

"How often did this update?" Grace asked. She was beginning to wonder how much they could expect from this experiment. Most of her ideas felt especially smart until she tried to actually enact them. This was beginning to feel the same way.

"Every decisecond," Yuka replied, her fingers typing in the air as she recorded some information in the network. "You should get most if not all of what you're looking for."

"Wow," Heron said with a teasing grin. "*Everything* I'm looking for*? Satisfaction guaranteed?*"

Yuka's expression faltered. "Excuse me?"

"Never mind him," Grace said. "He's a little excitable today." The table beneath her hand changed from blue to green, registering the implant in her proximal phalanx.

*<<Accept file RK7465#3*56?>>*

"Accept the file, and you should be good to go."

Grace saw Heron hesitate. "What's wrong?"

"Just scanning the file first," he said. "Can't be too careful with what you download into your head these days."

"All of our files are cleaned and compressed." Yuka's offense radiated from the cold glare she cast him.

"It's fine," he said with a tight smile.

"I'll leave you to it," Yuka said, straightening. "If you need anything, ping me on the building's server. You're free to use this room as long as you need, but I leave at sixteen hundred hours. After that, Ginna is your point of contact."

"Thank you for your time," Heron said quickly, but Yuka was already shutting the door.

"So you *are* human," Grace said.

He frowned at her.

"You're as prone to awkward social interactions as the rest of us. I was beginning to wonder."

"In case you thought I was an AI masquerading as human, let me state plainly: yes, I am flesh and blood. God, there are over four million files here. No wonder we needed implants."

"He stored three years of memories. At fifteen seconds each, that's about right," Grace said. She was already furiously flipping through Ravee's lenscape data.

So was Heron. With data processing as quick as his, he was ahead of her. He noticed her watching and gave a nervous grin. "Do you want to watch this in tandem or…?"

Grace surveyed the files' timestamps. "Let's start eight minutes before he was killed," she said. "It's thirty-two files up. That top one in the middle column. After that, I'll let you process the rest of the data on your own."

"You got it," he said, his eyes already flicking back and forth.

Grace initiated the first memory and found herself back in the lab where they had interviewed Dr. Cyrah. Deft hands adjusted the tubing to a sack, repositioning what appeared to be a liver in its casing and fluid. A few furious types on the lenscape where the data was logged, and then he was off to the next organ.

Once he reached the end of the row, Kapur looked up and surveyed lab fourteen. This section was empty except for Ravee himself. He seemed to regard the empty stools and bright table without purpose for a moment and then started on the next row.

"Too bad thoughts aren't recorded too," Heron muttered. "I would've loved to know what he was thinking then."

Grace gave some sort of noncommittal agreement to this statement. But in reality, she vehemently disagreed. She wasn't sure she wanted to know what someone thought in the moments before they died. If she had known Kaiden's thoughts, or Davion's . . . Would it have given her peace or even more grief than what she already carried? She was certain she knew the answer.

When the second row of data was only half logged, Ravee left the table suddenly. He exited the lab and walked down the lone corridor to the restroom at the intersection.

"Ew," they said in unison.

The exclamation had nothing to do with seeing a penis in Ravee's hand and everything to do with the fact that he had not *washed* his hands after urinating, before heading back to the lab.

"I hope you want a side of filth with your new pancreas, Mr. Salvatore," Heron said, shivering.

Then Lake was in front of him, hefting a bag up onto his shoulder with a wide, friendly smile.

Grace turned up the volume.

"Tom, how are you?"

"Good, good!" Lake replied. From this angle, Grace saw his eyes were a tad too wide. "Funny running into you. I didn't expect to see anyone."

"Are you back from—"

Lake didn't let him finish. "I'm in a different department now. Processing. End-of-day processing."

"Listen," Kapur was saying, almost as if he hadn't heard Lake speak. "I'm sorry about what happened with you and Sam. I told Cyrah that it was my fault, but she wouldn't listen."

"No hard feelings," Lake said, struggling again with the heavy sack on his back. "It all worked out in the end."

"I just feel bad, you know? I don't think you two should've taken the fall. These things happen."

Lake managed a nonchalant shrug despite the weighty sack. "It is what it is."

The sack, Grace learned upon further research, was specifically designed for cool storage transfer. It was used to transfer perishable goods in field locations where cold storage wasn't immediately possible. A strange but effective choice for organ theft.

"How is Sam?" Ravee asked.

"He's okay," Lake said, his expression stiffening around the edges. "I'll tell him you said hello."

Ravee leaned closer. "Has there been any improvement in—"

"How much do you think that sack weighs? Thirty-six kilos?" Heron asked.

Grace saw the panic blooming on Lake's face, presumably caused by the length of the conversation but also the weight of twenty-six organs on his back.

"Probably," she agreed.

Lake was speaking before Grace could answer. "If I don't get moving, I'll be in big trouble with my new supervisor."

"Right, okay." Ravee held his hands up in surrender. "Sorry to hold you up. Ping me sometime."

Then Ravee was opening the lab door. As soon as he stepped into the room, the door closing behind him, he stared at his feet for several minutes.

"Another place I'd love to have his thoughts," Heron bemoaned.

Though Grace couldn't see him now, she remembered the recording of Lake running down the hall and descending the stairs. She imagined that wretched sack bouncing against his back even as Ravee continued to stare at his feet, seemingly lost in thought.

Then his head snapped up at the sound of a machine-siren wail.

Ravee rushed through the stacks of metal racking to find the cause of the alarm. Several shelves were pulled out from their units and their internal trays laid bare. His hands fluttered like panicked birds as he pulled drawer after drawer out for his manic inspection.

At least twenty shelves had been emptied, their metallic frames gleaming with iridescent fluid rolling across their surface.

"Fuck," Ravee cursed before slamming the last drawer into place.

Then he was running out of the lab and into the hallway.

He did a full loop of the floor, and when he didn't see Lake, presumably, he seemed to decide on a different destination.

His panicked circling turned into a direct attack.

He threw open the door to an office and found Dr. Cyrah behind a desk, the blue glow of her lenscape active across her cheek.

"Lake was just here," Ravee spat. "He stole organs from the lab."

Dr. Cyrah stood slowly. She paused, seemed to consider something.

"He—"

"Shhh." Cyrah motioned him forward. "Follow me."

"You can't blame me for this again—"

"Be quiet," she hissed. "Not a word until I find some-where we can talk."

Ravee obediently followed her through the labyrinth of

rooms and labs in the Viscosity tower until finally she opened the door on a room Grace recognized.

"Here we go," Heron mumbled, recognizing the lab they visited the day before.

Grace checked the timestamp. Twenty seconds left. She exhaled, knowing what she was about to see.

Ravee whirled on Dr. Cyrah as she closed the door behind them.

"There's no monitoring in here," she said. "Now tell me again what you saw. What *really* happened."

Ravee ran a hand through his hair. "Lake was here."

"Lake was fired."

"That's not what he said. He said he was in the processing department."

"How stupid can you be? We don't have a processing department."

"You can't try to pin this on me. I won't go quietly!"

Grace saw the anger flash in Dr. Cyrah's eyes and how it transformed her face. "I brought you here to get your story straight. So get it straight."

"I didn't take anything!"

"I covered for you once."

"I told you I had nothing to do with *that*!"

"This is your last chance. When I open this door, I'm going to have to report something. Do you want to be fired like Lake and Crate? Do you want to go back to that shit-hole zone I saved you from?"

She took a step toward him, and another. Until her mouth was quite close to his.

"I won't ask again," she whispered. "Do you want this or not?"

The shift in her hips wasn't angry now.

"Don't," Ravee said, taking a step back. Then another. "I told you—"

"I told *you* that if you want to stay in this job, in this zone, you had better keep your promise to me. This is your last chance, Ravee."

"What about my promises to Risa?"

"Your promises to her? To *her*?"

Ravee turned away as if escaping the rage erupting from the woman. He turned toward the back of the storage room and ran his hands through his hair. "Loba, I—"

Ravee's vision blurred. The room around him shifted in and out of focus. His hand stretched out to grab the counter but missed. His body pitched forward.

When it flashed on again, he was on his hands and knees on the floor. Blood ran down from somewhere on the left side of his skull, splattering on the back of his hand. The lenscape was scrolling an error message along the bottom of the scape.

It flickered in and out twice. Then it blinked out altogether.

Heron and Grace met each other's eyes.

"Go back," Heron said. "Five files up."

"Why?" she asked. She thought the murderer was evident.

"I thought I . . ." His voice trailed away. "Yes, *there*. Look at her desk."

It took Grace a minute to catch up to him, to find the proper place in time. She froze the footage at the moment where Ravee had just stepped into the office and Dr. Cyrah's desk was in clearest view.

"Do you see it?" he asked.

Her eyes swept the tabletop again. On its surface sat a glass rod.

"Now jump to when he turns back to see if she's really coming."

Grace let the recording roll forward and then froze it again. Dr. Cyrah's dark hand was on the handle, but there was a gap between the door and its jamb.

The desk was bare now. The glass rod was gone.

Heron fell back against his chair. "Where is Dr. Cyrah now?"

TWELVE

THE RETRIEVAL UNIT was dispatched to locate and extract Dr. Cyrah from her lab. She cooperated until they bagged the glass rod on her desk. That was when she lashed out at the officer collecting the rod, trying to wrench it from his hands and dash it against the floor.

It was protocol enforced by the Nonviolent Extraction Act of 2282 that if a suspect began to resist arrest, they were to be immobilized with the simple KO tagger—a neurozapper that rendered them immediately and pain-lessly unconscious.

Since any act of excessive force resulted in immediate and permanent expulsion from the police force, Dr. Cyrah was delivered unharmed to the precinct, carried there by second-level transport with all the pomp and circumstance of a queen.

Back in the precinct, Dr. Cyrah lay reclined on a rose-colored sofa in the containment cell. This cell was one of 1,764 units in the building adjacent to the precinct. Each containment cell was four by four meters, with one wall projecting an endless forest or white beach—prisoner's choice—and basic pink furnishings. Pink had proven to subdue inmates when used in the correct ratio with white. The sofa converted to a bed. The table in the corner could seat two.

Heron and Grace stood watch over her, waiting for the medic to arrive and revive her.

"I can barely think in these rooms," Grace admitted. "They make me sleepy."

"She doesn't realize how good she has it," Heron muttered into his steaming cup of koffee. He put his koffee to his lips and sipped. "Jail cells used to be incredibly barbaric. They had a toilet in open view of a crowded cell and they didn't even have *seats*."

Grace snorted, disgusted. Sometimes she couldn't believe what sort of people she evolved from.

Heron took another sip. "And when we first started using the KO taggers in 2275, we were horrible at it. Police would zap you, and you could end up anywhere. Famously, in 2296, Thomas Tucker was KO'd while running away from police. They were in his manufacturing plant outside a city called Pittsburgh—"

"Where?" Grace had never heard of it.

"The area is part of Zone 16, I believe," he replied and took another sip. "And when he went down, he ended up falling off a platform and into the chemical vats below. He drowned in acid."

"Hell's bells," Grace said, grimacing.

"The judge ruled in favor of the officer that time. The jury said that had he not been running, it wouldn't have happened. It was his own fault."

"Justice prevails."

"Does it?" Heron snorted. "Two years later another law passed stating that we basically have to ensure that every suspect falls on feather pillows when we zap them."

Grace heard quick steps behind her and turned to find Domino Devani, the squat medic, rushing toward her. He waited for the containment cell to open for him.

"Domino," Grace said, motioning him in. "Thanks for coming."

"Commander," he said with a sharp nod. "I'm sorry about your family."

He blurted it as if he could only just keep the words in.

Grace managed a nod despite her tightening throat. "Thank you."

Domino opened his mouth to say something else.

"The suspect's there," Heron countered, and Grace was grateful that he'd stepped in and redirected the medic's attention.

Domino peered around them and marched to the side of the couch where Dr. Cyrah lay reclined in her rumpled lab coat. The medic with his hunched shoulders leaned over, cracking his knuckles.

"Back up," he told Heron, who was leaning over expectantly, as if he had never seen a revival before. Surely he had. As an inspector, he would have interrogated suspects at least in training, if not in the field. "Sometimes they come up swinging. Commander, are you recording?"

"Yes," she said. Every interaction from now until Dr. Cyrah's trial would be on record.

Domino placed his fingers on the back of the doctor's neck, in that little notch below the hairline. The fingertips on Domino's right hand burned a soft orange, warming like an iron in a fire.

Dr. Cyrah didn't come up swinging. Her big eyes popped open, and she swung her legs off the couch. She was sitting up, hand on the back of her neck, eyes furiously darting around the room.

"Where can I get me one of those?" Heron said, looking at Domino's fingers enviously.

"They're occ-mods," Domino said. "So you can get them by going to medical school."

Heron pretended to pout.

Domino held his fingers up in Dr. Cyrah's face. "How many?"

At first, she only looked at him. "Four." Her voice was thick.

Domino straightened. "A linguistic delay, but that'll wear off."

"Thanks so much for coming," Grace told him and turned away before she had to confront that sad smile.

Heron made the extra effort to stretch out his hand and offer to shake Domino's. "Wonderful to meet you."

Domino looked amused by this excessive friendliness but accepted the shake.

Heron's grin doubled. That's when Grace suspected he was up to something. The lingering handshake, the excessive smile.

Once the door closed, she gave Heron a wary look.

Heron wiggled the just-shaken hand at her, grinning at his fingers. He looked rather maniacal, actually. "Maybe later I'll tell you a secret about what this hand can do."

"I don't want to know what your hand can do." She thought of the sex worker, Arjun, exiting Heron's unit.

"Where am I?" Dr. Cyrah said, looking around the room. "How did I get here?"

"You're in a holding cell until your trial. Do you remember speaking with us?"

"Yes," she said, but she didn't sound sure.

Grace thought it best to go slow. "I'm Commander Buteo, and this is Inspector Jane."

Dr. Cyrah let her hands fall to her lap. "Have I been arrested?"

"Yes," she said. "For the murder of Ravee Kapur."

"I didn't do it."

"We have evidence to the contrary," Heron said.

"You can't possibly prove I hurt him." Then, as if realizing how this sounded, she added, "Because I *didn't* hurt him."

"Were you aware that Ravee Kapur had a memory storage account? The last three years of his life, up to the decisecond of his death, was stored on a private server."

The color drained from her face.

"I don't think she knew," Heron said. He seemed far too excited for a moment like this.

"When we . . ." She hesitated. "We had a lab failure last month, and he said he could prove he wasn't responsible for that."

"You didn't ask how he intended to prove it?" Heron rocked back on his heels.

"No." Cyrah shook her head. "I knew he didn't do it."

"Because you were responsible for the loss?"

Dr. Cyrah launched herself at Grace only to be slammed back onto the couch again.

"Our shields will remain up for the remainder of this interview," she said. "You can strike it all you like. Unfortunately, it often reflects negatively on you in court when the jury decides your case."

Cyrah's nostrils flared as her dark eyes fell to her lap.

She's looking for a way out of this, Grace thought.

"Your lenscape has been deactivated from the server," Grace added as confusion beset Cyrah's face. "You'll remain disconnected until a verdict has been reached."

Cyrah's chest heaved for several long breaths as she sought to control herself. And to Grace's surprise, she managed to do it. Good. She might have damaged her shield when she'd raised it against the bronze statue. She didn't want to see how well it still held.

"Memory banks record only what the eyes see," Dr. Cyrah said, finally. She searched Grace's face as if reading it. Then she looked to Heron.

"So?" he asked.

"You can't possibly have proof that I killed him," Dr. Cyrah said. "Whoever killed him hit him from behind."

"And *how* do you know he was struck from behind?" Heron asked, unable to hide his *got you* grin.

"I found his body," she said. "I saw the wound myself."

"I'm interested in the conversation the two of you had moments before Ravee died," Grace said. "You said, 'If you want to stay in this job, you'd better keep your promise.' What did you mean by that?"

Dr. Cyrah looked like she would be sick.

"What promise did Ravee fail to keep?"

"I need a lawyer," she said.

"Of course!" Heron said with a laugh. "But you also need to answer our questions."

He looked rather haughty in the corner of Grace's eye. Hands on hips, pelvis tilted like a cowboy's. Again, Grace wondered about Heron's training, his style, and whether she would ever get used to it.

"I want my lawyer," Cyrah insisted.

"If you won't talk about Ravee," Heron said, "what can you tell us about Sam Crate and Tomas Lake? You knew they were fired, yet you didn't mention them to us."

Dr. Cyrah looked ready to protest, but her face broke. "You saw them in the lab photo."

"And we saw them on Ravee's feed. That's what Ravee came into your office for, wasn't it? To tell you that Lake had appeared and now the organs were gone? Why did he assume Lake took them?"

"Lake and Crate were blamed for the loss and fired," she said. "It would be natural to assume they were responsible again if they weren't even supposed to be in the building."

Grace turned on her lie-detection program. "Why didn't you mention that two employees had been fired for theft during your initial interview?"

She said nothing.

"We came to the lab to find missing organs. Didn't you think it was a good idea to mention that—"

"It wasn't a theft," she said.

Truth.

"If you check Viscosity's records, you'll see that it was a machine malfunction."

Truth.

"It cost us fourteen organs, but we were able to replace those."

Unclear.

A half-truth, then. The question was, which half?

"If Lake and Crate didn't steal the organs, then why were they fired?" Heron pressed.

Dr. Cyrah looked at her hands. "Viscosity doesn't hire people who can't do their job."

Lie.

"So the lost organs were damaged, not stolen?"

"You can check the record," Dr. Cyrah said. "That's what it will say."

True.

"But is that what really happened, or is that just what's on the books?" Heron asked.

"That's what happened," Dr. Cyrah said.

Lie.

"So you didn't damage the organs on purpose trying to get Ravee fired?"

Dr. Cyrah's sputtered. "No."

Lie.

"And we're to believe that you didn't mention this organ loss or the fired employees because you didn't feel like it was relevant to the theft."

"Correct."

Lie.

"You think these two events are completely unrelated?"

"Yes. Absolutely."

Lie.

Grace nodded her head, knowing that the recording would also format the lie-detection results and add them to the data file.

"Okay, if it's unrelated, let's focus on why you're here. Why did *you* murder Ravee Kapur?"

Dr. Cyrah paled.

Grace was about to press the situation but saw Heron's blue light flash with incoming data. Then he turned to her and smiled.

"Commander," Heron said, conspiratorially. "Did you know that Ravee Kapur and Dr. Cyrah placed an application for a marriage license *four* years ago, but it was never completed? Kapur withdrew his request before the hundred-and-eighty-day holding period."

Grace arched her eyebrows and turned to Dr. Cyrah. "Is that true?"

The doctor stared at her lap, jaw clenching.

Heron didn't wait for her to speak. "And Dr. Cyrah left a note on his Viscosity application, vouching on behalf of his work ethic, and it was Viscosity that approved his zone visa."

"Interesting," Grace said.

"It seems like Dr. Cyrah did a lot for Ravee, and yet they broke up less than a year later."

"So his fiancée helps him get hired and transferred to a better zone, but then a year later they break up. And when he gets engaged to someone else—"

"Approximately fifty-four days ago," Heron inserts.

"—she starts planning to murder him," Grace finished. "Only it didn't begin with murder. At first she just wanted to get him fired."

"But when that didn't work," Heron said, "she got angry. Well, *angrier*."

"I did everything for him!" Dr. Cyrah screamed. Her face was transformed by her rage. Nose scrunched, lips pulled back in a snarl. "He used me! And he wanted to talk to me about his promises! Honoring his *promises*! How could he say that to me after everything I did for him? *How?*"

She collapsed into sobs, covering her face with her hands.

Grace let her indulge in the show for a moment. But only a moment.

"You put the glass rod into your pocket before you followed him to the lab, Loba," Grace said gently. "That wasn't the action of someone who killed in the heat of the moment."

When the doctor lowered her hands, Grace saw everything she needed to know in those dark eyes. Anger and fury, of course, but also what wasn't there. Remorse. Regret.

She was angry she'd been caught, not about what she'd done.

Dr. Cyrah squeezed her knees together and spoke in a composed voice. "I want my lawyer. I won't say anything else without my representative present."

Heron and Grace excused themselves without further comment. To do so would have been to break the law, or worse: have their information thrown out as coercion. The jury never accepted testimonies from suspects who were harassed into saying what they didn't mean.

So they closed the door behind them and breathed. Grace leaned against the adjacent door. The intimacy of the dark nook didn't escape her. Heron, too, seemed to notice. He took a polite step back and leaned against the wall, falling back into his own thoughts.

"Maybe she wasn't alone. It's possible someone slipped in right after her in those few seconds before he was struck."

"There was no one else," Grace said

"Does this connect to the organ theft?" Heron asked.

"No, I don't think so. To me, it seems like Loba saw an opportunity and took it. She probably hoped that the thief would be blamed for Ravee's murder," Grace said, watching the woman on the sofa, head in her hands.

"And what of the organs?" Heron asked.

"We have to keep digging," she said. *And see how deep this goes.*

THIRTEEN

"ARE YOU SURE IT'S HIM?" Grace asked, her disbelief palpable.

In her office, Heron shared his lenscape, reviewing the first pieces of footage returned by the spyders.

Heron licked his lips. "I suppose it could be his doppelgänger, but I doubt it. Crate has a rather distinctive chin."

Heron jutted his chin out comically.

Grace's mind began to curl up around the edges. "How can Crate be moving around a secure city without identification? You're sure he isn't registered?"

"No registration. No public or private identity. No clearances. Nothing except the expired tourist visa, which presumably, is how he arrived in the zone." Heron scratched his nose. "If he was picked up by patrol, he would be thrown on the Midnight Train and sent off to the stormlands."

She leaned back in her chair. "Yet he enters and exits a dozen buildings, one of which is bio-sealed."

"Correct," Heron said, fingers drumming on the top of her desk. "What do you make of it?"

She pressed her fingers into her temples. "Let's assume he came here on a tourist visa, let it expire, and began squatting in the city somewhere. How did he get a job at Viscosity? Where does he sleep? How does he eat? How does he *pay* for the food? For anything?"

Grace tried to wrap her mind around the idea. People couldn't wander around unregistered. Resource management simply wouldn't allow it. A secured zone was secure not only for the safety of its citizens. It was secure so that it could sustain itself and live within its means.

"Maybe he has friends or family supporting him," Heron suggested, following her. "There's no record of such a connection, but it's possible."

"No, we *know* Crate and Lake worked at Viscosity. Let's assume they were hired and sponsored as required by law, even though the record doesn't show that. Then it's clear they must've been deleted. Why would they delete themselves unless they were planning something radical?"

"Or Viscosity could've deleted them," Heron offered.

Grace shook her head. "That violates about fifteen laws and tax treaties. And if it could be done by someone in the company, by someone like Dr. Cyrah for example, Ravee would've been long gone."

She lowered the opacity on her office wall, and the street outside came into view. People strolled up the sidewalks, arm in arm. Some had extra sun gear on, suggesting the solar rating was up again. She saw a boy on the sidewalk, bright red pack gleaming behind him. He had puffy hair just like Kaiden's. Her heart stuttered in her chest.

"Commander," Heron said behind her. It seemed deliberately pitched low. "What are you thinking?"

She considered how to continue. Her voice was stuck in her throat, turning itself this way and that as if to dislodge itself. Then, at last, she found a place to begin.

Heron accepted her private chat immediately.

<<It was said that Lix Richards deleted himself from the system so that he could commit his act of terrorism and have a chance of escaping the zone without being apprehended. If Crate and Lake deleted themselves, maybe this theft is only the beginning. Maybe Crate and Lake and whoever they're working with have something worse planned.>>

Heron's drumming on the tabletop faltered.

"It makes you wonder how much time we have," she whispered. She wasn't sure if she was thinking about mortality in general or the impending threat of two unregistered men, walking around her city unchecked.

She closed her eyes and saw the four tires lifted from the pavement.

Kaiden's mouth opening in a surprised *O* . . . or had it really? She felt like every time she reimagined the scene, her brain mercilessly added a new, horrifying detail.

You could confirm the details, her mind accused. *You could replay that night, that moment.*

No.

The pushback was immediate and absolute. Unfathomable.

Let her mind jump at its shadows. She'd rather contend with those than the reality that was surely worse.

<<You think they're part of some network bent on breaching the zone's security?>> Heron asked. <<And Crate and Lake could be part of the same network?>>

<<The trial's final report said Richards was part of a radicalized group that infiltrated cities and caused discord from the inside. They did all this for the purpose of destabilizing them, so their resources can be harvested,>> she replied.

<<Do you believe it?>> he wrote. <<Do you really think that's the reason your family is dead?>>

She whirled on him suddenly. "Reason has nothing to do with it. There's no reason."

Heron waited. He watched her as if waiting for her to say something. Do something.

<<He said he didn't do it.>> She realized how tense her neck and shoulders were. She tried to relax into her chair. <<During the trial, Lix said that he was innocent.>>

<<You were at the trial?>>

<<No. I was in the hospital.>>

She gestured to her diminished face with her scarred hand.

<<But when I was released, I watched the trial's recording. His face . . .>>

No, not his face. What had horrified her most when watching the trial wasn't the look of innocence superimposed on Richards's features, though it had certainly unnerved her. It was how often the prosecution had used Grace's own name against him, the way they'd thrown it at him like knives.

Commander Buteo lies in a hospital now, fighting for her life, for a life without her husband and son, and you sit here, lying to us!

<<Did you think Richards was lying?>> Heron asked.

She wasn't sure she could answer. She turned back toward the people on the sidewalk again as seen through her transparent office wall. She thought about how the city carefully set aside enough water for each one of its citizens. Enough purified air. Enough housing and food. It strove to make sure everyone's needs were comfortably met. There was no poverty consciousness here. No fear of scarcity. And she saw that security reflected on the faces of everyone who passed.

No wonder the IED, and the death of her family had shaken them so badly. With lives like their own, they couldn't possibly imagine something like this happening.

"The lie-detection program said he was lying," she said aloud. *But about what?* she wondered.

"There isn't a lie-detection program in the world wiser than your own gut," Heron said as if trying to draw her back into the conversation. "Do *you* think he was lying?"

Another group of children ran by screaming, their faces wild with delight.

<<I can't imagine anyone would live here off-network willingly. Who would want that kind of life?>>

He laughed. It was a loud, sharp sound that felt more like a slap than laughter. <<You can't imagine why they would squat inside this pristine zone, stripped of privileges, rather than live free in the outer zones? Or hell, the stormlands?>>

She terminated the chat.

His face softened. "I am going to guess that you haven't been to the outer zones."

"No."

Whatever he was going to say next was interrupted by an alert from her lenscape. She opened the message and found that the spyder had returned with a live feed of the local community center for her. In the feed, she found Sam Crate entering the building, a backpack on his back.

"Come on. I know where Crate is," she said, out of her chair before the footage could even be fully reviewed. Grace ordered second-level transport for the sake of speed.

Taking the elevator to the roof, they stepped out into the warm day.

"I've never been in second-level transport before," he said.

Surprising for an inspector, she thought.

"Any plan to tell me where we're rushing off to?" he asked, stepping out of the elevator first.

"Crate is two miles away in the Hanscomb Community Center. We need to get there before he leaves."

They crossed the roof to the transportation platform. The transport slid open, receiving them a moment later. She gave the address she sought, and they were off before Heron even had a chance to sit.

"Oh, this is nice," he said, running his hand along the back of the seat. "This can hold, what? Twenty, thirty people in here?"

"Something like that."

"It's not a CityRide. It's more like a *Party*Ride." He smiled at his own joke.

Grace didn't sit. She stood at the panoramic window, reviewing the world that whizzed by. The rose-gold city seemed on fire in the late afternoon light. And in the distance, she saw the storms on the horizon, great crackling black clouds, illuminated by the electricity within. From this distance, Grace thought she saw the transformers darting in and out of those clouds, trying to capture and harness its terrible power. As enormous as those machines were, they looked no larger than flies in the distance.

"How far do you think that is?" she asked Heron, who now stood beside her.

"Fifty or sixty kilometers. I suspect it's over zone 98 or 99. Why?"

"The stormlands are supposed to look like that all the time," she said. "One large continuous storm, destroying the land."

"Yeah, that's what I've heard." The transport slowed, arriving at the rooftop of the Hanscomb Community Center. "Here we are."

Grace reluctantly tore her eyes away from those dark clouds and exited the transport.

The uppermost entrance was not bio-locked, so they entered the building without issue and went down to the main level. The elevator opened on a large desk.

"Hello there," said a cheerful receptionist. She was clearly AI. Grace could tell by the soft light in her eyes. "How can I help you today?"

"We're looking for a man," Grace said. "May I show you a picture?"

The AI accepted the photo offered by Grace's lenscape.

"Sixth floor," she told them. "You will find him in the mah-jongg room."

Inside the elevator again, Grace asked, "Have you ever played it?"

Heron arched a brow. "Mah-jongg? I have a beautiful set that my mother brought back from China. It was an apology gift for missing my graduation."

Grace marveled at this new information. China visas were the hardest to get. Its resource-management regulations were the strictest in the world. Grace had wanted to go there on her honeymoon with Davion, but their applications had been denied. The price of having one of the cleanest countries in the world, she supposed. "What was she doing in China?"

"They invited her to study the blue pitta, *Hydrornis cyaneus*," he said. "After a year of study, she was able to give the government her conservation plan and it worked. The pittas' numbers are healthy now. She loves it when that happens. Even more than the medal they gave her."

"Did you forgive her for missing your graduation?"

He snorted. "I forgive my mothers for everything. I was a difficult child."

The elevator door opened, and they stepped out onto the sixth floor.

"I think we'll find him through here," Heron said, pausing outside a large door.

"Do you have your KO tagger ready?" she asked.

Heron nodded.

"Good," she said. "I think there is a back exit to this room as well, so why don't you enter through here, and I'll go around the back?"

"All right," he said.

"Count to ten once I'm around the corner."

She counted along herself.

Ten . . . nine . . . eight . . .

. . . three . . . two . . . one!

Grace threw open the back door. Groups of four huddled around tabletop screens, their fingers furiously tapping.

Two men in the corner stood out. Their bodies were huddled, deep in their digital exchange. A pulsating lime-green glow on their ears signaled a shared private reality.

Crate was on the right with his recognizable chin.

Three strides, and Grace would reach him. But as soon as she turned in his direction, his light turned off, and his gaze snapped to hers.

He ran.

His hip clipped a table, making the mah-jongg game featured in its top flicker. Grace reached for him, but her fingers only grazed his collar. The rough fabric scraped against the pads of her fingertips before it was gone again.

He was headed for the door Heron blocked—the only other exit. Heron drew himself up as if to use the sheer mass of his body to cover the doorway.

Crate had a solution for that. He drew back his fist and hit Heron square in the mouth.

Heron couldn't have looked more surprised if he'd just received news of his own murder.

But the pain and surprise did the trick. Heron rocked back, stunned, and Crate was able to push through the doorway.

Torn between helping Heron and chasing Crate, Grace turned back to see that the man conversing with Crate had also run. He was gone, probably having slipped out the door behind her when she was turned.

"Are you okay?" she asked Heron as she stepped over him.

"He hit me."

"Yes," she said. "I saw it."

"He hit *me*. This *beautiful* face. He *hit* it."

She couldn't console him now. She ran. Down a corridor to a T.

"Go on then," Heron called after her. "I'll catch up to you."

She caught sight of Crate cutting a corner just a second before he disappeared. She tore after him.

She trailed corridor after corridor, until she turned down yet another hallway and was presented with the wide view of his back. Without pause, she fired her tagger and its prongs ejected from her device and sailed down the hall. They bit into his flesh and he went limp immediately, collapsing to the floor with an unforgiving thud.

FOURTEEN

AS GRACE WAITED outside a containment cell for the second time that day, her mind wandered to Davion again. She thought of the way he had looked as he stood before the transparent living room wall and watched Kaiden ride his bike along the sidewalk outside. She remembered visually tracing the line of his broad, dark shoulders, tight beneath his bamboo shirt, down to his loose hemp pants.

She'd come up behind him and encircled his waist with her arms. "How's our boy?"

"Determined to tear the skin off both his knees," he'd said with a low chuckle.

"I like determined men."

"And independent." He'd placed a cool hand over hers. "He refused my help three times. He insists on teaching himself how to ride it."

In her periphery, her son wobbled on his bike. His shoes slipped off the pedals and he tumbled into the grass. *Don't look,* her mind begged. *Don't look at him, not his face, or you'll fall apart. Memory or not, it will destroy you.*

She kept her focus away, turned toward Davion.

"Why me?" Davion had whispered.

"You were a stubborn, willful boy and this is your payback," she'd replied with a chuckle. Her face was buried in his warm neck.

He'd laughed. "Without a doubt. But I meant, why, of the thousands of people who apply to Zone 2 every day, should I be so lucky?" His voice had had a dreamy, far-off quality that had scared Grace. "Why *me*?"

He'd turned and looked into her eyes then.

"What did I do to deserve this house? This wife? That great kid?"

She passed a hand over his cropped, rough hair before cupping his cheek. "You were smart. You had the skills to—"

"None of that mattered," he'd said, cutting her off. He'd pulled her hands from his face.

His irritation had surprised her.

His melancholic moods were so rare they'd always unbalanced her. But he'd been human, and some days, his dissatisfaction simply bloomed like a rainstorm, its fragrance dark and electric, hanging around him every-where he went.

"There are *so many* talented people. People who've worked harder, people who need this life more than I do—there's no reason to think my merits exceed theirs," he'd said.

She'd wanted to say something to chase away those clouds in his eyes, but no words had come to her.

"It isn't fair, Gray."

"Lots of things aren't fair, but we do what we can to improve them," she'd said. "And if it were a choice between fairness and having you two, I wouldn't hesitate. I could never give either of you up. Even if it meant someone else would have a chance. I'd choose you every time."

Something she'd said struck him. His eyes rounded. His mouth opened, breath slipping through his parted lips.

Whatever he'd wanted to say next, he'd swallowed it down.

"I have to get to work," he'd finally choked out. His smile was forced. He'd left her standing alone in front of the transparent wall, watching Kaiden right his bike again.

How many arguments over meaningless grievances had ended much the same way? With Davion deciding it was better to close the conversation than open it up further and get at the thorn lying deep within?

It isn't fair, Gray.

As far as she was concerned, it still wasn't fair. Maybe it would never be fair.

Maybe *fair* was a word that fools threw around so they could sleep at night.

"Are you all right?" Heron asked. He was watching her shift her weight between her hips.

Her mind returned to the present moment and the containment cell before her. She regarded the unconscious man and wondered what was taking Domino so long to get here.

"I'm fine," Grace said.

"I'm *not*. Can you believe he hit me?" Heron said. He looked so indignant that Grace was laughing before she could stop herself. "How can someone hit *this* face? This isn't some moderated projection, this is my *actual* face."

Grace humored him with a pat on the arm. "Yet somehow you'll survive."

"Yes, but it makes me wish we were in the twenty-one hundreds."

"What happened in the twenty-one hundreds?"

"Everyone had those little chips I was telling you about. Police used them to subdue people remotely instead of shooting them with guns. If we'd had that, we could've pushed a button and Crate would've dropped. No punching."

These days, Grace couldn't imagine an officer getting away with murdering someone. None of the weapons they had now were capable of ending a life. They only immobilized. Detained.

"How did the chip implant work?" Grace asked.

"Just one remote *zzzppp*," Heron said, "and they went down. No need to chase them. No need to get within range. It was definitely easier on the hips. You could've sat here and pressed a button and they would've been waiting for you like Sleeping Beauty."

"Why did they ever do away with it?"

"Rights violations," he said. "It was ruled in 2288 that forced chip implantation was unconstitutional because it violated autonomy and due process. The presumption of innocence, not guilt."

Grace heard the heavy steps of Domino a moment before he appeared.

"Sorry, sorry," he said, bursting through the little door. "Here we go."

They followed the medic into the containment cell.

For the second time today, Domino placed his glowing fingers against the skull notch of their suspect and sighed. "I can't stay and chat. I've got about five more to do before the day ends. If he seems damaged up here"—he made a vague gesture toward his own head—"let me know."

And without further instruction, he was out the door again.

Grace hardly noticed. She was watching Crate's eyes flutter open.

"Hello, Mr. Crate."

He blinked at her. "Do I know you? You look familiar."

"My name is Commander Buteo."

He blinked several times. "Grace?"

Her heart skipped a beat, suddenly swelling and pressing uncomfortably against the base of her throat.

"*Davion's* Grace?" he asked again.

The room began to spin. "How do you know my husband?"

"I . . ." He searched her face and then turned to Heron as if just realizing he was there. "I, don't... uh . . ."

She leaned in, dominating his field of vision with her body. "*How?*"

His mouth opened and closed like a fish lifted from the water. Again, he glanced at Heron as if he would intervene somehow.

"Commander," Heron warned.

"Are you with Richards? Did you—"

"Commander," Heron said again. "*Lower* your voice."

That's when she became aware of her body again. Heron was squeezing her upper arm. Hard. It wasn't enough to bruise or hurt her, but enough to bring her back to herself.

Remember where you are, his eyes seemed to say.

The lack of control rolled within her, *there*, just beneath the surface. She'd been dangerously close to those blinding moments before she'd taken her defense stick and unleashed it on the bronze statue.

Here she was again up against the edge of it. She breathed.

Crate's eyes darted from hers to Heron's. "I must've heard about the accident on the bulletin. Broadcast far and wide, wasn't it?"

"You don't get the bulletin," she accused. "You're off-network."

A sharp knock on the door drew Grace's gaze. Commander Adams stood in the doorway, his face stern.

"I'm very sorry to interrupt, Commander. But do you have a minute?" he asked.

Grace felt the blood rise in her cheeks. "Of course."

She took a breath and stepped into the hallway, letting the door close behind her.

"I just heard you brought in another ghost. Is it true?"

Word travels fast, she thought. "It seems so. He isn't registered in the zone, and we can't find any public records for him in the network."

"Do you think he's connected to Richards's group?" he asked.

"I haven't established any connection yet."

"Are you sure you should be handling this?" Adams shifted his weight. "If this is the same case, you—"

She raised her hand. "I appreciate your concern. But I can't do my job if you intend to hover over me. As far as I know, this has a connection to the Viscosity case I'm working, and I intend to see it through. If it proves connected to Richards and more information can be introduced to *that* case, you'll be the first to know."

He clasped the back of his neck. "I know you can do your job. I know better than anyone. But the parallels between these cases—"

"There are no parallels. There's a coincidence at best," she said and wondered if she really believed this. "Why are you here? Do you have an interrogation?"

"No, I came to speak to you." Commander Adams took a step back, giving her an unblocked path back to the interrogation room. "I was asked to deliver a message."

A message that couldn't be delivered over the server? she thought but said nothing. She only waited.

"Richards was moved to a care unit last night."

Her throat tightened so quickly it was hard to squeeze out the next word. "Why? What happened?"

"He's on suicide watch. Apparently, he tried to end his life."

"To avoid exile to the stormlands?"

"That's not all. He's made his final request."

She braced herself for what she already knew was coming.

"He asked to see you."

FIFTEEN

TASTE OF THAI, a restaurant in Low Town had amazing fried curry fritters. They were the best in the zone, in Grace's opinion, but her ChefMate had made a nearly identical replica of the dish. Grace thought of the delicious little pockets as more like curry *puffs* than anything as chewy as the name *fritter* suggested. But she ate heartily nonetheless, dimly aware that her mother would be ecstatic to see her appetite returning.

The delicious spices and fried bread dissolving in her mouth was the closest thing to real pleasure that she'd experienced since waking in the hospital. And because her mother hadn't had the courtesy to recalibrate the machine to a serving size of one person, it had made plenty.

Despite the delicious oil she wiped from her lips, Grace's mind kept drifting back to the Crate interview. Or, rather, lack of interview.

Once she'd stepped back into the room, he'd refused to speak. No matter her questions, he remained silent, eyes fixed on some distant point only he could see.

Exhausted and more than a little angry, Grace had excused herself for the day.

But coming home and eating one of her favorite meals hadn't brought her the focus she'd hoped for.

Perhaps it was her blatant disregard for the calorie watch's suggestions. She'd opted instead for the heavier, less nutrient-dense fritters, and now exhaustion pressed itself against her mind, muffling her thoughts and senses.

Davion's Grace?

Crate had known her husband. And if he was off-network—and they knew he was—there was no way he had heard her story from the bulletin. She had been *Davion's Grace*, not *Commander Buteo* as undoubtedly she'd been called every time her name was blasted to every corner of the zone.

Of course this almost certainly meant he was part of Richards's terrorist cell. Preliminary evidence supported this theory, and yet she hadn't wanted to tell Adams. Outside the containment cell, when the opportunity sprang up to bring Adams into the loop, she'd pulled the lie between them like a curtain. It had been instinctual, and now she wasn't sure why.

When did she stop trusting Adams? He'd been one of her staunchest supporters in the precinct. He'd campaigned on her behalf for the position of Commander. He'd been her friend and confidante for years…so what the hell just happened?

"What are you doing, Gray?" she asked herself as she lay on her sofa staring at the digital sky above. It offered no answers.

Synthetic clouds floated lazily by.

She knew she wasn't supposed to go anywhere near Lix Richards or the bombing case. It was a conflict of interest. But she found she couldn't give up Crate either.

How long could she get away with digging before someone noticed?

Just as Grace wasn't sure when Adams had become untrustworthy, she also didn't understand her newfound affection for Heron. There was still something off about him. The way he acted in the second-level transport, as if he'd never ridden in one before. His surprise at Crate's strike, as if he didn't know that suspects often lashed out.

The look on his face when Crate had said *Davion's Grace?*

She kept turning that look over and over in her mind. Yes. Something was happening. It had not come completely into view for her yet. The connections weren't clear. But she sensed the shadows shifting in the dark around her and knew that soon—very soon—someone would turn on the light.

A creak caught her attention. She sat up on the sofa and noticed for the first time the front door was open. Had it been that way before? Would she have noticed when coming through the garage?

Grace pushed off the sofa and activated her spatial scanner as she went. It removed the opacity of every wall and corner to reveal the rooms behind. It gave officers the chance to see if anyone waited to attack.

The first floor of her unit was empty.

No one stood in the kitchen or open living room, clear all the way up to its high ceiling and open sky above. She looked through the upstairs floor and thought she saw the shuffle of feet.

Feet. In her bedroom.

She removed the KO tagger from her pocket.

It took no time at all to cross the living room to the stairs.

She mounted them two at a time and rushed past the closed bathroom and into her bedroom.

As soon as she saw the man standing there, she thrust her KO tagger into his neck.

Nothing happened. He didn't lose consciousness or collapse. He didn't stir or flinch.

That's when she realized it was the Boi. The bot wore a pair of loose pants and stood in the bedroom facing the dresser.

"Hell," she swore. "Call Mom."

Her mother answered the call on the third ring.

"What the hell, Mom?" The words rushed out of her in a single breath.

"What?" her mother said sheepishly.

"Why is this damned bot wandering around my house?"

"Oh, I turned him on so he would clean your house. *You're welcome*."

"He isn't cleaning. He's standing in the middle of my bedroom, scaring the hell out of me."

"He was supposed to put himself back in his closet when he was done. Mine always does unless something has interrupted him."

"And you left the door open."

"What door?" her mother asked. Grace heard the creak of a cabinet.

"My front door."

"I did not," she said, indignant. "I made sure it was locked up tight when I left."

Grace's heart jumped like a rabbit in her chest. Had she left the door open? No. She was certain she'd come through the garage.

She turned and caught something in the corner of her eye. A man ran down her stairs full tilt.

"What's wrong?" her mom asked, responding to Grace's sharp intake of breath.

"I'll call you back."

She was already on the stairs when the call ended.

He was here this whole time. While she ate, while she lay on the couch musing, dozing. *He could've come right up and . . . what? Killed me?*

But he hadn't. And he was running away faster than Grace could keep up.

He was out the door and onto the street before she reached the living room.

On the pavement outside, she looked in every direction, but nothing. No dark hair. No black jacket and pants. The sidewalks and streets were empty except a woman walking her dog toward the community path.

She pinged Heron.

"Someone was in my house," she said before he could get a word in.

Only he still didn't say anything.

Grace realized it wasn't his face that she was seeing but a live feed share. He'd given her access to his lenscape instead of saying *hello*. Why?

She froze on the sidewalk, looking down on Heron's bare chest, down to the hem of his pants. At the blood.

"Heron?" she asked, heart hammering.

For a horrified moment, she thought she was looking at an accident. Maybe he'd been hurt and this was a call for help.

But then Heron looked up, and in the frame was Lake's face.

Lake stood over him. Lake adjusted his grip on the knife in his right fist.

"I see him," she said, hoping it would be some measure of comfort. "I'm coming, Heron. I'm coming. Hold on."

SIXTEEN

IT TOOK Grace only a moment to decide she would go alone. She could call for backup, but she'd seen Lake on Heron's feed. Lake, an unregistered man. Calling backup now meant there was a real possibility the case would be removed from her care. The promise of truth would be lost.

So no backup. Not yet.

Lucky for Heron, Grace still had access to his locked housing community, and the CityRide auto was able to drop Grace off in front of Heron's whitewashed unit. She crept up the walkway leading to the front door, and turned on her scanner, hoping to sweep both levels and get a sense of where the assailants were so she could prepare her counterattack.

<<Scan block. Password?>>

She frowned at the unit and tried again.

<<Scan block. Password?>>

She hadn't been prepared to find a firewall. Of course, she wasn't surprised. This was Heron. His gadgets seemed to afford him levels of privacy she'd never imagined. But this meant she had to enter the house blind with nothing but her KO tagger and defense stick.

If we die, it's your own fault, she thought. This of course assumed that Heron wasn't already dead. She couldn't be sure what Lake's intentions were in assaulting an assistant inspector. Nor could she be completely certain that the intruder she'd found at home was on Lake's team.

She pushed the front door of the unit and found that it opened easily.

Because they want you to come in, she thought and pulled her tagger from her pocket.

She crossed the threshold and stepped into a foyer.

A high chandelier of crystalline light hung above. Heron's unit was laid out much like her own. The kitchen sat straight ahead, but no ChefMate arm hung beneath the cupboards, poised over a range top.

No one waited in the kitchen or behind the front door. No one squatted under the small table for two. She kept moving, finding herself in the spacious living area. It rose to the full height of the unit before revealing a luminous sky. It was a program like hers, giving a perfected version of the sky free from particulate haze.

A large electric fireplace crackled in the corner beside a rug made of synthetic fur. The wall-length windows on all sides gave the room considerable light. One wall also had a forest program running, replacing the view of a neighbor's unit with a dense forest full of creatures scurrying from the undergrowth and leaping from branch to branch. Then there was the birdsong.

It was hard not to be distracted by the simple but breathtaking embellishments of Heron's living space— until she saw the foot. Or rather she saw a black shoe protruding from behind the sofa. She crossed without hesitating and found Heron sprawled there, bound and gagged on the floor.

She swore and turned him over to undo the bindings at his wrist.

His eyes opened halfway.

"Hold still," she said. Her hand had grazed his bloody chest and now her palms were sticky with it. "I'm almost—"

Heron's eyes came into focus and he flicked them over her shoulder. His chin lifted ever so slightly. She began to turn but was too slow. Something cool touched the back of her neck.

Then the world went black.

WHEN GRACE NEXT OPENED HER EYES, SHE SAW HERON sitting opposite her, his back against the wall beside his stairs. His chest was cut and bleeding, but the wound didn't look as if it had been made with a knife. Otherwise, he was unhurt.

She was gagged and bound. The base of her skull ached. Whatever they'd used to knock her unconscious hadn't been a KO tagger. She'd revived on her own and there was none of the cognitive dissonance associated with a tag. And it *hurt*.

Her desire for the truth wasn't so great that she wanted to get Heron killed. *Or yourself,* some voice added. *You don't want to die either.*

She would argue that point later.

She tried to use her out-call feature to signal the precinct that they were in trouble. Nothing happened. She tried again and her lenscape began to change.

It flicked twice and an electronic notepad opened on its own. Then script appeared as if by magic.

It's Heron, the script wrote. *Sorry for the intrusion.*

She tried to reply and found that it wouldn't work. Her thought-to-text feature seemed to be disabled.

Heron turned and showed her his neck. She saw the thin, silver medallion stuck to his skin. It was fixed to the tender meat where the lenscape processor was usually inserted subdermally.

You have one too. I believe it's the BD prototype. They disable all lenscape communications except for this tiny oversight I'm now exploiting. I have an override program, but it's limited in its capacity, so I can only do so much. I can talk to you, but I can't give you back the features of your lenscape. Sorry. I'll try to ask only yes-or-no questions. Okay?

She nodded.

Let's see how good I am at guessing what you want to know. You probably want to know who they are and where they are now.

She nodded.

It's Lake and another man. No name on him yet. They're upstairs, going through my bedroom. I'm sure you want me to send a message to the precinct to get help.

She nodded.

I could, but listen. I have another idea. This would be a wonderful chance to be damsels.

She arched an eyebrow.

I've always wanted to be a damsel. I can tell by the look on your face that you're not interested in my proposal, but this might really work to our advantage. Let them think we're pitiful, and then BAM, we take the upper hand.

Or end up dead in a shallow grave, Grace thought, and she wished she could say that. She wondered if skepticism and downright irritation was coming through on her face as clearly as she felt it thrumming in her bones. If it was, Heron didn't seem deterred.

By appearing weak, I think this is our chance to get information that Crate wouldn't give us. We have to be brave enough to endure a little hardship if it means bringing the enemy down, right? Ever been tortured?

She cocked her head.

Me either. BDSM, sure, but I don't think that counts, he replied. *Rather controlled by comparison, isn't it?*

Grace didn't want to know how Heron preferred his sexual pleasures, but it was too late. The image of Arjun dominating him was already blazing in her mind.

Her eyes slid to his bloody chest. She tried to point at it with her chin.

He looked down as if seeing his wounds for the first time. *Oh, I'm fine. This was me, actually. When I caught them, the other guy pushed me, and I hit my glass lamp. It shattered as I landed on it. I think his knife is only for show. We're about to find out.*

Feet on the stairs made them both look up. Lake was in the lead, the other man behind him. He had a weaselly face with a pointed snout, inverted-triangle head, and protruding ears.

"You have only the one safe upstairs, and given it only had *this*, I'm sure you've got another one hidden around here somewhere."

I have four safes, actually. He'll never find them.

This, Grace saw, was a set of black rings encasing each of the man's knuckles. The knuckles device was illegal, mostly because it would fry someone's brain if the power was turned up, not to mention split skin and shatter bone. She wasn't sure she wanted to know where Heron had gotten it.

Forget what I said about torture. Heron never took his eyes off the device. *I've called for help.*

Grace spoke, but the words were absorbed by the swath of cloth in her mouth. Lake turned his attention to her.

"What's that, my dear Commander?" Lake asked, almost amused.

She looked at the gag, then met his eyes.

"Have something to say, do you? If you scream when I remove this gag, I *will* test it on you." Lake held up the electronic knuckles, the black metal gleaming.

She nodded, conveying that she understood.

He pulled the cloth from her mouth, leaving it cotton dry and burning in the corners.

"Where are the organs?" she asked.

Something flickered in his eyes. He looked disappointed. "Gone. I've sold them all to the highest bidders. So forget about getting them back. And you're going to make sure my friend Crate is released. Now."

He pressed the charge button on the device and it hummed. He pressed it against the side of her throat so she felt the vibration.

"I'm going to take off the BD, but if I don't get a notice that Crate is being released in four minutes . . ."

Grace only looked at him. Four minutes was impossible. No one could notify him that quickly unless he had someone inside the precinct.

He misunderstood her contemplation for resistance. He lifted the knuckles and pointed them at her. "I've always wanted to see if the rumors that they liquify the eyes is true."

Grace still did nothing.

Grace? Heron asked.

I can't give him what he wants.

I don't think this is like a game of Tide. Out or in, he will zap the hell out of you.

"Four minutes," Lake said, searching her face.

"I want to know who you sold the organs to."

"And I want you to release my friend," he said.

Friend. Not business partner or associate. *Friend.*

He must've seen something flicker in her eyes. He pressed the knuckles into her throat harder. She felt her throat click as she swallowed.

But she wasn't afraid. Her limbs weren't heavy. Her stomach wasn't sick.

She was here. *Now.* But she wasn't afraid.

That was one good thing about losing everything she cared about. The fear left her too. There was nothing this man could take from her. Nothing worse than the whites of Davion's eyes as he leaned over to cover their child. Nothing worse than the confusion and fear filling Kaiden's face.

"How did you delete yourself from the network?" Grace asked.

Lake laughed. "You think I deleted *myself?*"

The man behind him laughed too. But there was no humor in their voices.

"Do you really think any of us blacklisted *ourselves?*" Lake lowered his outstretched arm, removing the device from her neck. "I heard you were smart, Commander. I must admit, I'm disappointed."

Help is coming, Grace. Keep him talking.

Grace resisted the urge to look at Heron.

"Since you obviously have no idea what's going on, let me enlighten you. No, we didn't delete ourselves. We were happy to remain law-abiding, tax-paying citizens. Until we were *erased* to improve a company's profit margin."

"The zones have strict resource-management requirements. If you were fired, you should've been compensated with other opportunities, or at least a chance to—"

"A chance!" Lake hissed. His face crunched into a

hideous snarl. "Oh yes, they offered us many chances indeed! We could go to the outer zones, places worse than where we came from, or we could disappear, have our own organs harvested for those cold, storage racks."

Her heart pounded in her chest. Maybe all the fear hadn't left her after all.

"Have you ever been to the outer zones? Do you know what *a chance* looks like out there?"

She said nothing.

"They're starving. Their skin is rotting off their bones from sun exposure, and their water is too filthy to drink, either from the rain that pollutes it or from the viruses that can kill the drinker. The worst of them eat each other. What in the *world* makes you think I would go to that shithole willingly? Why would I condemn my wife and daughter to a life out *there*?"

"We should put her on the Midnight Train," the other man said to her. "Maybe then she'll get it."

"We could." Lake's face twisted up as if he liked this idea. "Would you like that? Ride until dawn on a trash heap bound for the incinerators? You'll have *a chance* to ride right into the fire or jump off and live with the rest of the no-zoners."

The other man opened his mouth to speak, but his body jolted suddenly. His face screwed up, then he fell. He crumpled against the sofa like a drunkard. Lake only managed a half turn before he also seized up. He fell to the floor, revealing the tall and beautiful Arjun with his sandstone skin and liquid black eyes. His long hair had fallen forward, framing his face. He looked like one of the ridiculous heros on the cover of her mother's famous romance novels.

She looked away.

Heron seemed to understand her discomfort. *Yes, he's turned on his Radiance implant. It usually dazzles people. It would slow their reactions in case they fought back,* Heron wrote into her lenscape.

"Turn it off," she said aloud. "And get this blocker off my neck."

Arjun's beauty became bearable by the time his fingers brushed her throat.

"This is the help you called for?" Grace said. She should've said it over a one-way chat so as to not seem ungrateful to her rescuer. But she was furious. She wasn't sure why, but she was shaking with anger. "We have proper protocol in this precinct—"

"I thought you wanted answers." He was unperturbed by her anger. "If you take Lake into the precinct, he'll go silent like Crate. This way we might actually solve this."

Arjun was helping him to his feet and undoing the bonds.

She bit back her anger and tried to convince herself this was some of Heron's brilliant, out-of-the-box thinking. But her adrenaline was falling fast, and with it came the crash of emotion.

"This isn't about organs. Something is going on here," Heron said, hissing as Arjun inspected the cuts on his bare chest. "Don't you want to know the whole story?"

She did. God, she *did*.

"Give her a minute to think, bird," Arjun said, his hands on Heron's chest. Heron rolled his eyes up to meet Arjun's.

Grace couldn't bear the look shared between them.

"May I?" Heron asked, offering to remove her bonds. She acquiesced. She just needed to think. She just needed a minute to wrap her head around all of this.

Arjun pulled Heron around the corner and out of sight. And for a moment, Grace was alone with herself, if she didn't count the two incapacitated and unconscious men at her feet.

Don't you want to know the whole story? he'd asked.

Beware the story in a story, Davion had said to her once.

She'd been leaning against the kitchen counter, forking dollops of crème into her mouth after they'd put Kaiden to bed. She could still feel his hand on her hip.

Why?

If you stop at the first ending you come to, you might think you know the whole story. But what if it's only the first turn—part one of three? You have to follow it all the way to the end, excavate all the threads, or you'll never know what you're really looking at.

Her memories pressed in on her. Four rubber tires lifted off the street. The auto's frame screamed as it was engulfed in flames.

What was she looking at? Could this lead to answers she wanted? Not about this damned case, no. Organs and identity fraud, sure.

Those were the answers she would get if she called the precinct and had these men hauled away to containment cells. They would be arrested for the theft, tried, found guilty, and expelled from the zone.

But who took the organs and why, were only two questions—and they weren't the questions that kept her up every night, replaying her husband's memories as she caressed his cold pillow.

She'd woken in the hospital bed, body aching to the belief that an unlisted, radicalized man had wanted to kill her. This attack had not been personal, but he wanted the death of the zone's commanders and officers to send a message to the governing body he detested. And maybe in that vulnerable moment, his comrades could overtake the zone for themselves.

Then, in a separate case, she discovered that two unregistered men—bearing much resemblance to the terrorist that tore her life apart—have stolen organs. One knew her husband's name. They called her Grace.

And it was more than that. There was the fact that they hadn't really hurt her, not yet. They hadn't hurt Heron. They were angry and resigned, but they weren't…

You think we did this to ourselves?

Beware a false ending.

No.

She couldn't stop now. She had to know.

And wasn't that her privilege as commander? Wasn't she allowed to dig as deep as she wanted to find the truth?

Grace stepped over Lake's unconscious body and retraced Heron's steps. She wanted to tell Heron her decision and see what tools he might have to help them.

At the door, she hesitated at the sound of low voices.

"I'm saying you *like* her." Arjun spoke softly. Grace was able to appreciate the sweet vibrato of his voice. It was smooth against her ear.

"I do. I mean she's a *little* penal code, but what's not to like?"

A long silence followed.

"You like her even though she can lawfully chain you to the Midnight Train. She's your commander, not your friend."

"I gave him my word," Heron said. "I'm *here*, aren't I?"

Grace stepped around the corner and made her presence known.

Both men turned to look at her then. Grace forced a tired smile. "You're right. If we bring them into the precinct prematurely, we won't get a chance to discover how all of this is connected. I think these men knew my husband and might know more about what Richards was up to."

"There," Heron said with a smile. "It all comes down to the truth, doesn't it? It's the truth we want."

"Yes," she said, her gaze steady on Heron. A new possibility unfurling in her chest. "Yes, it is."

SEVENTEEN

HERON CLAPPED his hands together and rubbed them like a villain as he regarded the two unconscious men. They were strapped to chairs at the foot of his bed: a pair of blue wingbacks, the linen upholstery pristine.

"You are enjoying this too much," Arjun said, pushing the hair away from his face. He stood to the left of a bathroom door. "You're scaring the commander."

Heron only briefly flicked his eyes up to consider Grace's face. "How can you say that? She's a seasoned professional. She's done hundreds of interrogations."

"That's an exaggeration," she said, hoping her steady voice hid the fact that she *was* worried.

A general sense of dread was building inside her. She was afraid of what they might say, or not say. She was afraid this was a terrible mistake that might result in real repercussions, possibly a suspension. And she was afraid that Heron would betray her—even if he'd said he would never. How did she know he couldn't override a lie-detection program if it served him?

Stay focused, she told herself. *One problem at a time.*

You're bothered because you're such a rule follower, Grace, her husband used to tease.

And that wasn't enough to save you, was it?

She pushed back against the bitter thoughts and tried to concentrate on the room. She looked from Lake to his accomplice. She regarded the deep royal-blue coverlet behind them on the enormous bed that Heron surely shared with Arjun. Every night? Every other night? *And with who else?* she wondered.

"Ready?" Heron asked, searching her face.

She found her voice. "I want to be clear. We're using only pain compliance methods, no actual puncturing of skin or anything that would cause lasting damage."

"Oh no," Heron said with a manic smile. "We don't want them to have any visible evidence of torture to present in a court of law. Of course not."

She wasn't sure if she was comforted or horrified by his excitement.

Arjun arched his eyebrow at her. "Heron gets like this when there's danger."

"With all due respect," she began, "I'm not sure you should be here. I certainly wouldn't have let Davion remain present for a . . ." She searched for the correct word.

"Delicate moment?" Arjun offered.

"Business."

"I'm only the muscle," Arjun said, palms out in surrender. "I'll be the one to carry the bodies to the auto when you're done with them. I can step out if you prefer to work without an audience."

"There will be no *bodies*." Grace's heart turned in her chest. "But you can stay. As long as everyone understands I'm in command here. If I think anything has gone too far, you *will* stop on my command. *Immediately.*"

"Yes," they agreed without hesitation, and Heron and Arjun shared a nervous smile.

Heron then turned that beaming grin on her. "Ready? Okay. Let's wake these beauties."

A sharp *zap* of Heron's finger sounded as he touched Lake's throat.

Grace's mouth fell open.

"Yes, I copied that feature when I shook Mr. Domino's hand," Heron admitted. "I have a replicator chip in this hand. I can duplicate anyone's embedded software if they shake with me long enough."

"And what did you steal from me?" she asked. Though they'd brushed the backs of their hands in a profile share, hadn't they? Was that the same?

"Nothing." He winked. "Much."

Lake gasped as if rising out of cold water.

"Hello, how are you?" Heron said, again too cheerful.

"I'm fine, thank you," said the man mechanically. Then, as if he realized he was strapped to a chair and at the mercy of the people he'd been threatening just moments before, the terror set in. "Wait—"

"Can't, sorry," Heron said. "My commander is a very busy woman, and I promised her I'd keep this quick. So I've got all four of my data processors running on this."

Four, Grace thought. No wonder he seemed to have her questions answered before she could think them. What a fortune must be implanted in that neck of his. He had better hope he was never captured by scavengers. They would strip him for parts.

"So that we're all on the same page, let's recap. You're Tomas Lake. Private first class. You did three domestic tours and one overseas in aid dispersal. You came from Zone 168. Not the best zone, but not the worst either. I'm sure nutritional issues account for your short stature and the titanium leg."

Without meaning to, Grace looked down automatically.

"My body scan says you've had quite a bit of mod work, actually. The leg, but also lung filters and . . ." Heron walked around the chair, squeezing between the end of his bed and the chair itself, and surveyed the man from behind. Arjun watched in amused silence. "Is that a moisture moderator lining your spine?"

"These are survival modifications," Grace said, frowning at the freckled man. "Did you get them during your service?"

Tomas laughed, bitterly. "I needed them long before that if I didn't want to end up thrown into Plowman's Field."

She didn't understand the reference.

Tomas seemed to relish her ignorance. "In Zone 168, we have a fallow field outside the edge of town. It's where we heap the bodies."

Her stomach turned.

"Here you have beautiful Soul Groves. I've seen the trees you plant over your dead's ashes and the sweet little plaques with their embedded holograms to preserve their memories. We have to cover our dead with dirt and etch a few words on stone. Leaving them out in the sun to rot leaves a stench so foul it saturates the air for kilometers. You smell it in your hair, in your nose, on your skin. Even if you could get your hands on enough water to bathe, no amount of scrubbing takes the stench off."

Grace's throat was so tight she wasn't sure she could draw a breath. It wasn't just the story Tomas told, which was horrible enough. It was his face. The *hate*. The contempt for her in this man's eyes was thick enough to cut. Is this why her husband was killed? Did these people from the outer zones really resent them so much?

"My son and my husband are in a Soul Grove," Grace said, thinking of the beautiful inscribed forests running through the northwest part of town. She didn't tell him that she hadn't been able to bring herself to visit the wide, grassy avenues where the mournful were invited to wander. Not yet. "What was left of them, anyway. What . . . they could pull from the burning auto."

Emotion flickered across Tomas's face.

"Do you know anything about that?" Grace asked. She didn't care if she sounded angry. Or if she sounded hopeful. Heartbroken or rolling in complete and utter despair. The time for being self-conscious about her emotions had passed. "Because Sam seemed to know exactly who my husband was."

Tomas looked from Grace to Heron, who was coming around the chair again. He looked like a man who realized that this wasn't a simple interrogation. When it was personal, the rules seldom applied.

"Davion was your husband." It wasn't a question.

Grace's heart skipped a beat. "Yes, and our son, Kaiden, was with him when the auto exploded."

"Fuck," he said. His eyes fell to his lap.

Grace turned on her lie-detection program anyway before asking, "Did you kill my family?"

"No."

"Did your people? Your . . . *organization*? Were you trying to send a message to authorities or—"

"No," he said. "We weren't responsible for that."

Truth. At least as far as Tomas knew.

"Don't be shy," Heron teased when Tomas's head drooped. "What do you know about the auto explosion?"

They should be asking about the organs, about details

pertaining to the Viscosity case. Why was Heron indulging her?

"We don't know who was responsible."

Lie.

"You're lying," both Grace and Heron said in unison. They cast each other sheepish sideways glances.

"We have suspicions, but no facts," Tomas amended.

Truth.

"Why only suspicions?" Heron prodded.

"Because who would talk to us? We're nothing, less than rats." Blood rushed to Lake's freckled face. "All I know is they wanted Davion stopped, so they stopped him."

Grace staggered. "Are you saying Davion was the target? Not me?"

"I don't know," Tomas said, his face earnest.

Lie.

"*Davion* was the target? *Davion*?" Her voice exploded from her. "No. *No.* He was the kindest. He was the—"

"We don't know if he was the target. It could've been you."

Lie.

"—the most loving and *no one* would want to hurt him. *No one!*" His attempts to deescalate her had come too late. Grace had his shirt in her hands, rending the front with bunched fists. She yanked him up so hard that the chair came with him, the front feet dragging along the carpet of the bedroom floor.

"I'm sorry," Tomas said, squeezing his eyes closed. "I'm so sorry."

She dropped the chair, and Tomas slammed into the ground, eliciting a surprised cry as the chair legs rocked.

Heron was righting him when Grace stepped forward again. She wasn't even sure what she meant to do, but she had her KO tagger pointed at his right eye when two strong arms lifted her and spun her away.

Three big steps and Arjun had her out of the bedroom and at the mouth of the hallway.

"Let go of me!" she screamed.

He did so immediately, but his large body remained in the frame of the door, blocking her path.

"Take a breath," he said.

"Don't you tell me what to do!"

"I'm sorry," Arjun said, moving to block her path. "I can't let you back in until Heron says it's okay."

Grace got a look under Arjun's outstretched arm and saw Heron's mouth moving. He was continuing the interrogation without her.

"I'm the commander. He's my inspector."

"I'm aware. But this is his house," Arjun said. Grace expected cold indignation at her petulant tone, but all she saw was compassion. "And you've just heard that your husband might be the reason your son is dead."

"My son." Her body went limp in his arms. "No. No, Davion would never."

But already her mind was seizing the idea, like a spider, spinning it up in its silk threads, wrapping it tight.

Her mind began its inventory. It gathered all the little things Davion had said. All the little lies he'd laid down here and there in the last fourteen months of his life.

Are you having an affair? she'd asked one night after dinner. After she rinsed uneaten salad leaves from her bowl and put it in the dishwasher, the question had escaped her lips.

No, he'd replied with a laugh.

Truth. And in that instant, she'd felt silly for using an interrogation program on her own husband.

Drugs? She'd asked anyway, as if she had no shame. *Any secret addictions?*

He'd quirked a brow at that. *No.*

Truth.

She'd been ready to drop it then. If he had secrets, it wasn't about her or their marriage.

Why the questions, Gray? He'd slipped his arms around her, placing a kiss on the side of her neck.

I just have to ask every once in a while, she'd said weakly. *How else will I know if I don't ask once in a while?*

He didn't laugh at her lame joke. *What are you worried about? Are you sensing danger around the corner?*

She'd turned and looked him in the eyes. *Do you keep secrets from me?*

No, he'd said.

She hadn't even needed the lie-detection program to tell her this was a lie.

You're the one I trust most.

Truth.

I don't want to keep secrets from you.

Truth.

"Do you have any reason to believe Tomas?" Arjun asked gently. He was leaning against the bedroom door now, watching her.

Why in the world would she believe anything that came out of Tomas's mouth? He was a thief at best, a terrorist at worst. Who knew what other crimes he might have committed?

"My husband was a good man. He was a loving husband and an amazing father." Her voice broke on the word *father*.

"He could be those things and still have a secret," Arjun said, as if these thoughts hadn't just crossed her mind too.

A ping popped up on her lenscape. Heron had messaged, as if he hadn't been the one to throw her out in the first place. <<Come back in when you're ready.>>

Arjun must've gotten a similar message, as he stepped out of Grace's way without having to be told.

<<There's nothing else to be learned about your husband from this one,>> Heron told her silently. <<I think we—or you, rather—really will have to speak to Lix Richards if you want to know what happened that night. Or at least what they think happened. Either way, I believe Tomas when he says that they're not responsible.>>

"Tell her what you just told me," Heron said aloud, not taking his eyes off Tomas.

"Yes, we took the organs," he replied mechanically.

"For?"

"For the displacements that we take care of. When they need medical attention, we have to do whatever needs to be done to see that they get what they need. Some of them were ejected from their jobs specifically because it was no longer cost-effective. Often, for medical reasons. So many of them come to us quite sick."

"What do you mean *displacements*?"

"That's what we call them. Displacements."

"Them who?"

He looked genuinely surprised. "All the people we take care of. Everyone off network. Our entire community."

"You're terrorists. Your numbers can't be more than twenty at most." *No more than forty in this whole city*, she added, but only in her own head. These people were exploiting the weaknesses of a system, exploiting it for their own political and monetary gain, but it wasn't a broken system. No way that many people were moving around this zone unregistered.

Tomas looked from Grace to Heron to Grace again.

"Tell her," Heron insisted.

Tomas licked his lips. "We have thousands."

He said it quickly, almost apologetically.

Grace felt the air leave her. "No."

"There are *thousands* of people in the underground," he said. "Literally thousands."

"Impossible."

"When the companies that sponsored our visas determined we were too expensive to keep, they deleted us. They pulled us from the system and threw us away. Our names, our homes. All our possessions and citizen rights were struck from the record overnight. Most of us had false tourist visas planted in the system so that if we were picked up, the police would think we're squatters. But we aren't. We're displaced."

She shook her head. "If that happened, someone would report it. They'd file a suit against the company and demand retribution."

Tomas laughed. He looked to Heron as if she'd just made the biggest joke in the world. Grace looked to Heron, too, and didn't see disbelief. His strained smile was part fury, part heartbreak.

"Commander, why in the world would we ask for your help?" Tomas asked. "The second we showed up at the precinct, we would be arrested and deported. Hell, that's what happened to Lix."

"Richards was arrested for murdering my family, not for asking for help."

"He went to the parade hoping to catch one of the officers on the street, to talk to them in a crowded setting so he could get away if he felt unsafe. *Surprise*, he didn't find anyone willing to listen. He got arrested."

"What proof do you have to corroborate this story?"

"Are you listening to me? There's nothing in the system

to verify our identity. Even our pretransfer lives have been deleted. We don't exist. That's why deportation is so terrifying. With no proof of prior citizenship, even in our old zones, we have only one place to go."

The stormlands.

Grace's jaw was tight. "You did that to yourselves. You're hackers. You needed to be ghosts so you could get into the system and tear it down."

Tomas laughed, a loud, indignant bark. "Why in the *hell*—do you even know where they send undocumented people? Do you think we could survive there? Raise *children* there?"

Children.

"If someone deleted you, you could've come forward with proof."

"What evidence could we possibly have?" he asked.

"You have that photo." She briefly described the photo they'd seen in laboratory fourteen.

"A work photo." Tomas laughed so hard that his seat rocked. "You think I can take a photo to court and win a case against a company like Viscosity? Are you kidding? You can't be so naïve."

Her face heated.

"They deleted us, our families, so they could balance a budget and widen a profit margin. That's it, and there is no way we could prove it in a court of law. They rendered us powerless, and they know it. I can't even make you believe it. *You.*"

He was right.

She couldn't believe it. She absolutely couldn't accept that thousands of people had been thrown away. It was criminal. It was worse than criminal. It was a human rights violation. It defied the system they built to protect and serve all the lives they could. The central zones were supposed to offer shelter to as many outlanders as possible. It's ultimate goal was to have no one in the stormlands.

To provide futures for everyone they could sustain. Not throw them away for *money*.

Each calculation for the resource management was dependent on the companies doing their share to protect the people they promised to protect. If they were really widening their profit margins by throwing away people—it had to be stopped.

Over her heart pounding, Grace managed to squeeze air out of her lungs. "Show me."

EIGHTEEN

HERON OPENED HIS GARAGE, and Grace discovered that there was a private auto in it.

"Is this yours?" she asked. She touched the machine as if to be sure it was real. It wasn't a plain standard-issued auto like the one she'd had before the explosion. A compact, economical auto. This was beautiful. A metallic blue, long, sleek and large enough for several people.

It must have cost more than both their living units and furnishings combined.

She'd forgotten about Tomas at her side. Heron had put a network blocker on the back of his neck, and if he tried anything, the man would be disarmed before any harm could be done. They'd decided to leave the accomplice unconscious for now. Better odds to have three against one.

Arjun, who was indeed proving to be the muscle in this situation, stood by the auto with the unconscious man slung over his shoulder. His legs hung down the front of Arjun's torso.

"Yes, it's mine," Heron said, walking up to the side of the machine. "But no need to mention that to anyone."

"Why?"

He only gave her a look as the auto reacted to his proximity and opened.

"Welcome, Mr. Blue," the auto said as the four of them maneuvered themselves into the auto. Grace sat beside the unconscious man, and Tomas was put between Arjun and Heron.

Mr. Blue, Grace thought. *A secret name for a secret auto—come on, Grace. How much warning do you need? Heron isn't who he says he is. How do you know he isn't friends with the enemy? How do you know they aren't going to take you somewhere now, torture you, and kill you?*

Hell, what kind of name is Heron?

"Where can I take you today, Mr. Blue?" the auto asked.

"Tell her," Heron said, speaking to Tomas. Grace noted the affectionate use of *her* when referring to his auto. It reminded Grace of her mother and the way she spoke of her Boi.

"Ninth and Bush," Tomas said tentatively. He looked squeezed and nervous between the two men.

"That is not a registered destination, Mr. Blue," the auto replied in her pleasant lilting voice.

"We're going anyway," Heron said. The auto locked its doors, issued seatbelts, and, once they were fastened, backed through the open garage door.

Knock, knock. <<Accept private chat with heronjane1? >>

Grace accepted the private chat with Heron despite her growing unease.

<<If you haven't guessed, this is an unregistered auto.

It's off-grid and untraceable. I only use it if I want to go somewhere without the network knowing.>>

<<You get more and more suspicious the longer I know you, Heron. Are you sure you aren't a criminal?>>

His lips quirked as he tried to suppress a smile. <<Would you mind if I were? Is there a rule that you can't solve crimes if you commit them? I think it would make me rather good at it. The solving part.>>

Grace only stared at him, and Heron's good humor stiffened. Worry darkened his eyes.

Tomas didn't notice. He was too enamored with the auto, looking at its custom interior and wide windows as if he'd never been inside one before.

Grace understood. The custom auto *was* far nicer than the most elegant CityRide, from the electric lights along the bottom to the dark tint that gave the impression of privacy and seclusion. The CityRides, too, were private, with reflective glass on all sides protecting those inside. But this was different. Not much of the world was visible around them, a small, intimate space.

Heron licked his lips. <<I think you should know, before we go into the secret lair of some undocumented squatters, that I *do* have something to tell you, Commander. And should we survive this, I promise to do so.>>

She recalled the whispered conversation between Heron and Arjun in the hallway.

Maybe it wasn't that Heron deliberately kept secrets from her. Maybe it was only that he didn't trust her yet. And why should he? He'd only known her for days, and when considering that, Grace saw objectively that he'd been incredibly open with her. Despite their difference in rank, despite their newness to one another, he'd told her things that she would have never shared.

He'd given her far more than she'd given him. And she knew it.

The tightness between her shoulders relaxed and she afforded him a smile, as much of a smile as her diminished face would allow.

<<I'll make sure you survive then,>> she told him.

He straightened and some of his confidence returned.

Arjun must've been aware of their private conversation. He was watching her face too, or at least until he politely looked away and engaged Tomas in conversation about his family.

Grace casually flicked her eyes back to her lap. <<Is it something I will have to arrest you for?>>

A long silence followed. So long that Grace finally looked up to find Heron smiling at her. No, grinning.

<<Perhaps.>>

She didn't know what to say to that.

<<Can you just—>>

<<Sorry, Grace, but your curiosity will have to wait.>>

She understood. They couldn't be far from this underground city—if there was an underground city. If this was as big a reveal as Heron seemed certain it was, he couldn't tell her now and walk away to attend the case. It would have to wait.

<<But I can tell you that if you want to drag women and children screaming from the underground just because they're undocumented, I won't help you. In fact, I'll deter you by whatever means necessary.>>

She supposed that his means were considerable.

But despite this challenge, she wasn't angered.

<<I wouldn't do that.>>

His smile only widened. <<I know. It's one of the reasons I like you.>>

She wanted to argue that it wasn't possible. That in no way could he know her well enough so soon. A couple of days with her, no matter how eventful, wasn't enough to know her. Not really. It took years to know someone's thoughts and character.

Even then, one could never be sure . . .

She thought of Davion. *Do you keep secrets from me?*

The auto slowed. It turned from the main boulevard down a side street. The slow glide down an alley between two buildings gave her no sense of where they were. She saw only walls on either side. It was so tight a second auto couldn't pass.

She recognized this part of town though. It was comprised of distribution warehouses for manufactured goods. Concrete buildings with no windows.

"There's nowhere to hide an auto," Tomas said, craning to look out the windows at the narrow street and buildings on both sides. "If you—"

"It's okay," Heron assured him. "I'll send it away."

"Will it come back?"

"I control it remotely. It'll come when I call it."

Tomas's shoulders slumped with either resignation or relief. It was hard to tell given the nervous way he continued to work his bottom lip with his teeth.

"I'll carry him in," Arjun added, nodding toward the unconscious man sandwiched between Grace and the door.

"Or he could walk?" suggested Grace.

"Right, right." Heron reached over and brushed the man's throat with featherlight fingers.

His eyes fluttered open instantly. He looked from Grace to Heron, and then, as he began to comprehend what had happened and where he was, his eyes widened and panic set in.

"It's okay," Tomas said quickly beside him. "It's fine."

"What the hell are you talking about? What—"

"We're going to see your little underground city," Heron said in a chipper voice. "Tomas has promised us a tour."

"*What?*" the color rose in the man's face, turning it an alarming scarlet. His black eyes shone.

"Relax," Grace said. "We aren't going to hurt you or your people." *If you have any people.*

"She doesn't believe we really have a whole city beneath the city," Tomas muttered, as if saying it low would encourage the man somehow.

"You're putting everyone at risk. If they raid, if they—"

"I trust them," Tomas said.

"You're an idiot," he hissed back. He lunged and wrapped his hands around Tomas's throat.

Another light brush of Heron's hand against his neck and he collapsed, his head falling into Tomas's lap.

"So…I'll carry him?" Arjun said, his smile a little wider.

Tomas rubbed his neck, grimacing. "Good idea. Oppa is a good man. He's just cautious. He has a lot to lose. We all do."

The auto slid to the end of the alley, and Tomas undid his belt. "Here. This is a good place to slip in."

Without hesitation, Grace, Heron, and Arjun unbuckled their belts and stepped out of the auto. It took Arjun a moment longer to pull the other man from the vehicle and position him over one shoulder.

Tomas watched him with unease. "He's just worried about his kids and—"

"He'll be fine," Heron said, clasping Tomas's shoulder. "Arjun has excellent hands."

This is the most lively he's been, Grace thought. *Because he's starting to show me who he really is.*

Without a word, the auto door closed and sped away down the alley. Grace turned to Heron to make sure it was intentional.

"The auto will ride around until I call it. It's self-charging, so it can run for weeks if we decide to become honorary members of this little community," Heron said, giving Grace a wink. He turned to Tomas. "I'm sure you need a commander and inspector down there. Who solves your crimes?"

Tomas didn't answer.

Heron kept pace with the shorter man easily. Grace, too. Arjun brought up the rear, casting glances behind him and around the narrow street. He seemed to be following orders given silently by Heron. Her suspicion was confirmed when Heron gave Arjun a knowing look. Arjun looked ready to burst out laughing.

"Here," Tomas said, stopping at the side of a building.

"Here where?" Grace said. There was only a street beneath her feet and a wall in front of her.

"Clever," Heron said, stepping forward to press on the wall.

Under his touch, the door gave, moving to the side to reveal a metal staircase that led down into the darkness.

"There are no lights. You have to run NightLite to see."

This was no problem for Grace and Heron, who'd come with the standard-issue programs afforded to all officers. But Arjun stood on the dark step, motionless.

"It's just the entrance," Tomas assured him.

"Or we fall down and break our necks, and then you've eliminated two nosy officers and one foolish bystander," Arjun said. He adjusted Oppa on his shoulders.

"Now, now," Heron scolded him. "We can't be accusing our new friend of treason. Yet. Also, you're no bystander, my love. Give yourself more credit."

"Take my hand," Tomas offered.

Heron clicked his tongue in mock outrage. "*I* will do the hand-holding, thank you."

"He's the jealous type," Arjun said, accepting Heron's outstretched hand.

"I really am," Heron agreed.

Slowly, they descended into the darkness. Grace relied on the digital outlines of her NightLite program to reconstruct the steps for her despite the consuming pitch.

Then a door opened.

Light poured forth, and Grace took a sharp intake of breath.

She stepped into the underworld and was overwhelmed with the wonder of it.

For an underground city, it was full of light. Bulbs and lanterns ran the length of the enormous cavern. Makeshift buildings, more like pop-up tents, lined a wide avenue as far as her eyes could see. There was music somewhere. It wasn't synthetic but sounded as if it was made with strings. Joined by soft voices.

People.

So many people. Thousands, surely. Maybe *tens* of thousands if this place truly did stretch the length of the world above.

It really was a city.

"Behold," Tomas said dramatically. "Our city of ghosts."

Grace couldn't count how many faces she saw, of every age. But many seemed to skew older. Then she heard the laughter of children.

Children.

Erased children. Forgotten children. Ghost children forced to live in this shadow world.

"My god," Grace whispered.

"Do you believe me now?" Tomas asked. "We aren't terrorists, Grace. We were erased. Displaced. I'm telling you that all the corporate sponsors are doing it. They don't care about the lives they destroy. They care about their profit margins. And no one checks them. No one is making sure they are fulfilling their tax contracts with the zone. They're going to tell you we're terrorists, but we're not."

"No," she said, stepping forward. She couldn't stop looking at the children.

As they walked down what could only be described as a center thoroughfare, Grace couldn't believe all that she saw. It was like a bazaar. Food stalls and vendors. People standing around talking. Eating. Laughing.

"How do you get all of this down here?" she asked.

"The underground shipping lines are just up there." He pointed at the dark above. From her place on the ground, Grace could see the faint outline of the delivery tubs crisscrossing in every direction. "Everything ordered from a household account travels in those lines. You purchase furniture for your living room or toiletries for your bathroom, it goes through here. You restock your fridge or need new sheets, we know about it first. Everything is boxed up by the robot AIs in the plants above and sent through the underground until it arrives on your delivery platform at home."

"You're scavengers. How brilliant," Heron exclaimed. "I love it."

Tomas seemed encouraged by this praise. His embarrassment receded. "Yes, but we only take what we need. We don't want to be caught and shackled to the Midnight Train. By limiting what we take, the companies think a poorly calibrated machine simply missed an item. No harm done. They resend that item to the buyer with little cost to the company and none to the buyer, thanks to mass production. We keep careful track of what we've taken from whom and when so we don't overdraw."

In a zone with a million consumers purchasing millions of products a day, Grace could see how such an enterprise worked.

"Down here we run by barter and trade," he said. "Some of us are able to get items from above, from friends or family who were blessedly left in the system or by using our old connections to get items from secured buildings."

"So, did Dr. Cyrah know about this city? Ravee Kapur? Anyone at Viscosity?"

"No," he said, his voice firm. "We protect this city's secrecy with our lives. It's all we have."

And yet you told me. They'd put their entire lives at risk, their own small slice of peace and security, by showing this place to her.

"Then why would you tell me?" she asked.

He only looked at her. Then he did a curious thing that Grace kept replaying in her head for days after. He looked at Heron as if to confirm something. It sent a chill through her.

Do you keep secrets from me?

"We want your help, Grace. We want you to hold the companies accountable, to stop them," Tomas said. "There has to be a way to stop them. Everyone here *earned* their place in this zone. They can't do this to us."

<<What companies don't know about the rats in the building?>> Heron pinged her.

"You can put him here." Tomas motioned to a chair beside an unmanned food stall. Arjun slid Oppa off his shoulders into the chair. "I'll wake him up later. After you're gone."

"He'll be thrilled, I'm sure," Heron said with a wry smile.

Relieved of his guard duty, Arjun began up the thoroughfare, his eyes swinging left and right to take in all the stalls.

Heron tracked his movements.

Arjun stopped in front of a man cooking something over an open fire. Grace could smell the meat from here. The cook scooped something from the pan into a folded tortilla. It looked like fajitas. Arjun paid for the meal with the shirt hugging his chest.

He returned, shirtless, and handed Heron half of his food. Heron accepted it with a smile, his eyes openly sweeping the man's chest. "You're undressing and handing me food. This is a win-win situation if I've ever seen one. And you still have pants. After this I want some dessert. Where are the dessert stalls?"

No one humored him with an answer.

"They're *good*," Arjun declared, his mouth full of fajita.

"Hell yes, they are," Heron moaned around his own first bite. "Maybe I should donate my fortune to the underground and enlist. Would you take me?"

Tomas didn't seem to hear. His eyes were fixed on a distant tent. Then he met her gaze again.

"Come on," he said, waving them forward.

Not a tent, Grace realized as they approached its exterior. Up close, she saw it was a field unit. Or rather a row of fifteen units, their off-white canopies looking like tents. A field unit was a sterile environment that could be constructed out in the open for the purpose of medical procedures. Usually they were only used for emergency situations where the external environment could not be trusted to prevent infection. Bacteria and viruses were rampant in the outer zones where the climate was less controlled. All the muggy warmth provided the perfect breeding ground, and the lack of clean water helped transference.

Grace reached forward and pulled back the flap on one of the tents. She stared through the sealed, clear plastic chamber at the surgical platform within. A full mechanical table lay brightly lit and bare.

"You just put people on the tables, and it performs whatever procedure you need?" she said, wondering if she'd been on such a table as her arm was reconstructed.

"You forget that these people were professionals," Heron said around a mouth of sautéed meat. "They *were* the surgeons and the table techs."

"I worked in surgery," Tomas said quietly beside them. "I oversaw all the cardiac surgeries, and was on a team with twelve other cardiac surgeons responsible for calibrating and maintaining the machines for each procedure."

Grace saw a little girl run by, pulling a kite behind her. It would never fly down here. But how could Grace explain that to her? That what she wanted was impossible in such a place? That the game wasn't *drag the canvas behind you while squealing in delight*? Was she even old enough to know what she was missing? How long had she been down here? Had she been *born* down here in the dark?

Tomas was still talking. "Then one morning, Viscosity quietly decided it didn't need thirteen cardiologists. They kept only three surgeons responsible for facilitating the organ transfers and ghosted the remainder. We're all down here. With our families."

"How did you cope with your loss?" Arjun said

tenderly. His dark eyes were soft and sincere in the lantern light.

"Some of us found a new purpose. I threw myself into work. There wasn't much of a medical unit before we—me and Lake and the other Viscosity rejects—showed up. We built all that you see here and keep adding on when we can. When Sam and Oppa showed up, we had the idea of full organ transplants, only possible on the MedX4000 tables. Then we got two of them. We don't require a lot of transplants, but we do have a need. Mostly, we see vitamin D deficiency down here. I suppose I don't need to tell you why."

Grace lost sight of the little girl with the kite. In her place, a dog trotted by. It was sable brown with his right ear folded, the other erect. He had a happy trot as he followed the scent of the girl.

"You have dogs," Heron said, eyes wide. He sucked the last of his fajita from his fingers.

"You'd never believe what people try to dispose of," Tomas said glumly. "Someone had put him in a disposal sack at the waste-drop site north of Pendam. We were scavenging the lot and heard him whimpering."

Grace wasn't surprised to hear they visited the drop lots. The city encouraged its citizens to visit the drop lots in the name of conservation. *Finders Keepers*, the motto went. While some enjoyed it, she knew that most citizens were too busy to be bothered by such a hunt. Why spend an afternoon sorting through dropped goods when you can request the specific item you desire in seconds and have it waiting on your delivery platform for you by the time you got home?

She'd only been to the drop lots twice herself. Once because Kaiden had a report for school, and he wanted to see it for what he called *his research*. They'd spent nearly an hour wandering the open lot, looking at the discarded items. Clothing. Scuffed shoes. Blown-out appliances. A chair with two missing legs that could only lie on its side. He'd dutifully inspected each item, taking notes with his dictation program. He'd called her over from time to time when he'd found something fascinating. All the while, only quiet stretched out around them. She'd seen a few others at the other end of the lot, bent down to inspect their prospects. Had one of them been from the city of ghosts?

The second time she'd come to the lot was only because her recycle chute had been nonfunctional that week. She hadn't seen anyone that time.

"You aren't worried about being spotted above ground?" Grace asked.

"No," he said. "No one ever pays attention to us."

"You took the organs for the people here?" Grace asked.

"Yes," Tomas said. "We have a little blind girl who is a match for the eyes we took. Two men needed the hearts. A woman had a failing liver. I could go on."

She didn't know why, but shame welled up inside her.

"Why wouldn't Crate tell us?" she asked.

"Crate's daughter is the blind girl," Tomas said gently, as if he knew that the news would wound her somehow.

"I'm sure he'd sooner give up his life than hers," Heron said. He was trying to get the dog to come over for a pet. The dog was bouncing back and forth, initiating play. "He wouldn't want to take the chance of us confiscating the eyes or pulling you out of here."

Tomas agreed. "He blames himself for their situation. Thinks maybe he wouldn't have been let go if he hadn't made a mistake in the lab that ruined some of the organs. Since the accident and his dismissal, Henna's changed. Henna is his daughter."

Grace now knew it had been Dr. Cyrah who'd made the lab mistake in an attempt to frame Ravee. Would that knowledge make a difference now? No.

"How has she changed?" Arjun asked. The dog had come to him instead of Heron, and he was smirking gloriously about it.

"Before they moved down here, she'd had no problem with being blind. And why should she? Blindness is simply a different sensory experience. That's how she felt too. Except after they moved here, Henna changed her mind. She wanted the eye transplant. Sam blames himself for that. He sees it as a sign that bringing her down here made her feel too vulnerable."

Grace couldn't do anything but stare at the city. At the bazaar, at the rising shipping containers that Grace now realized had been converted into living quarters for the displaced people and their families. Despite their hardships, they'd found all they needed down here in the dark.

"So what will you do?" Tomas asked. "Can you help us?"

Heron was watching her too now. And Arjun. They waited for her to make some proclamation about their fate. He'd made his case, his plea, and now he waited for Grace to decide: salvation or damnation?

"They're going to want to know where the organs went in our Viscosity report," Heron pressed. "What shall we say?"

Grace saw the dog chase after the little girl with the kite, her footsteps echoing in the dark.

"The truth," Grace said. "We tell them the truth."

NINETEEN

GRACE STOOD on the sidewalk in front of Viscosity Inc. and used the building's vid cam to confirm that her team was in place. With the constable's approval, Grace overrode Viscosity's security network and entered, bypassing the AI.

This is rather exciting, isn't it? Heron pinged. He was to her left with his defense stick drawn as they made their way to the stairwell. *Will our job always be this exciting?*

No, she replied. It was a trend she could do without. But even as she told him this, there was a small lurch in her chest, what felt like a warning of things to come.

She kept a unit of five officers waiting outside the elevator with KO taggers at the ready.

Do you think he'll—

Focus, she chided him. *If this goes poorly, you'll never make it to the bar for happy hour.*

And our overdue conversation, she thought to herself. In the report and coordination, they hadn't had the time to sit down and have the conversation he'd promised her.

It would have to wait until tonight.

She took the lead on the stairwell, up to the penthouse floor to find one Getty Peters, head and CEO of Viscosity.

Her heart pounded with the exertion as she reached the top floor, but her pace didn't slow.

When they exited the stairwell, only one door confronted them at the end of the hall. Grace hoped they would enter the inner sanctum and find a calm and cooperative Getty behind his desk. They'd disabled all communication going in and out of the building to ensure that he wasn't warned of their arrival, but Grace knew firsthand that all of this preparation meant nothing.

Living was the ultimate surprise.

Grace pressed a hand to the cool door and pushed it open. Getty stood behind his desk with a syringe in the throat of a sobbing receptionist.

It was the same blonde receptionist that Grace recalled meeting on her first trip to Viscosity, the one whom Heron had shamelessly flirted with before learning he was under the watchful eye of his commander.

Tears streamed down the front of her face. Red marks shone up and down her arms. She must've put up a fight before. But now she stood very still against Getty's chest, her left cheek bruised and swelling.

"You're assaulting her," Grace said calmly, though her insides were on fire. "Remove the needle from her neck."

"No." Getty snorted, his black eyes blazing, nostrils flared. Color burned in his cheeks. "Step away from the door and let me pass."

"Where do you think you're going to go?" Heron asked. It seemed like an honest, sensible question. "We've impounded your auto, assuming you could even get to the garage below. Every exit to this building is sealed. You can't possibly get out of here even if we did move out of the way. And I don't want to spend the rest of the day chasing you around this building. I'm tired just from climbing the stairs."

He sounded petulant. An interesting tactic.

Grace stepped toward Getty.

As she expected, he turned toward her, sensing danger. They locked eyes.

"Give them the order." Getty's hands shook. "Tell them you made a mistake. Tell them to leave."

"Do you even know what you are being arrested for?" Grace asked. She hadn't yet declared the charges.

He hesitated.

"It could be for any number of crimes then?" she asked with a cocked brow. "In addition to the fact that you're assaulting this woman and resisting arrest?"

"You must've been a very bad boy, Mr. Peters, if you're not worried about a little assault on top of it all," Heron said.

"What are you here for?" Now Peters sounded almost hopeful.

"We came to charge you with fraud."

Fraud of? his face seemed to say.

Grace filled the silence. "You've unlawfully fired 1,066 of your employees from your company. It violates your business treaty with the zone and also human rights code 312. I'm sure there's some tax evasion in there as well."

Getty's pupils ate away the color of his irises. "You can't prove that."

"I can," she said and smiled. "I gave enough evidence to the constable this morning to earn your warrant, didn't I?"

Heron made his move. Now in range, Heron shot his projectile tagger. Peters ducked at the last moment. This was the receptionist's chance to run and she did, swatting the syringe from her neck. She didn't even stop once she reached the doors. She kept running.

Let her go, Grace commanded the two dozen minds linked to her own. *We'll get her statement later.*

Grace's business was with the man in front of them. It would've been easier if Heron's tagger had incapacitated him, but no matter. She wasn't leaving without him.

"I made a mistake requesting you," Getty hissed. He came around his desk, inching toward her. "I thought I was asking for a shell-shocked, pathetic woman. But look at you. The other one would've done as he was told."

Adams?

She pulled her tagger the same instant he lunged. He knocked her to the ground, collapsing on top of her.

She felt the unnatural weight of his body pressing into hers.

Heron was behind him instantly, trying to wrench his arms but it was of no use. Peters was stronger.

Grace's right arm—the bionic arm—pushed back against Getty's chest, shoving him up and away. With his free hand he was groping for something, slapping at the ground until his face lit up with victory.

A needlepoint loomed in her vision, sparking in the light. He'd found the damned syringe and was now trying to stab her in the eye with it, his full weight thrown against her braced arm.

The bionic arm was unfazed. It bore the weight easily. Her very human shoulder, however, began to ache.

"You ugly, burned bitch! I told them we shouldn't keep you alive," Peters hissed. "I told them it was a fucking mistake!"

Grace tilted her hip and brought her knee up, driving it into his groin. His body seized and he rolled, collapsing onto his right side, the needle still in his hand.

Grace pulled Heron back instinctively. He was too close.

"I fucking told them!" Peters laughed. It was a wild, crazed laughter. "And look at you now. You have no idea what you've done."

He swept the room with wide, panicked eyes before his gaze landed on her.

"They'll destroy you for this," he said.

Grace saw the danger too late.

"No!" she darted forward, arms outstretched.

But in that instant, Peters plunged the needle into his own neck and depressed the plunger.

Grace caught him under his arms as he was falling.

No! No! No!

Live, damn it! She thought. *Live and tell me what the hell is going on!*

But there was no use.

The light faded from Peters's eyes, the hollowed gaze fixed on a ceiling he could no longer see.

TWENTY

APART FROM THE dead body of the defamed CEO Getty Peters, Grace removed only two other items from Viscosity. Wrapped in paper to hide it from view, Grace carried the large rectangle out to the level two transport vehicle waiting for her. The other item, taken from Peters desk, remained secretly tucked into her pocket.

Heron, Grace, and twenty-three other officers entered the vehicle. The post-operation jitters buzzed in the air as miniature conversations erupted around them.

Grace received their gratitude for a successful operation in which none of her officers died. She tried to accept this graciously despite the cold fact that Peters was quite dead—and with him, the answers to questions that she now knew had formed in her mind since she woke aching in a hospital bed.

When she wasn't replaying Peters last words, her thoughts flittered from distraction to distraction. No one seemed to notice. Most talked and cheered and laughed as the vehicle traveled five times the speed of the autos they sailed over.

<<Do you think this will work?>> Heron asked her in a private conversation. He was looking at the wrapped item in her hands. She wasn't sure he knew about the secret in her pocket. That item would not go into any reports.

<<If it doesn't, we'll try something else,>> she replied.

He smiled at that. <<I like you, Grace.>>

She frowned at him.

He laughed aloud, causing the passengers closest to him to turn toward him curiously. "My apologies," he stuttered. <<I won't make the mistake of accosting you with my affection again.>> "I'm watching my cat videos on replay. It helps me to de-stress from stimulating encounters like the one we've just had."

<<I've been to your house. You don't have a cat,>> she said.

<<Shows what you know. She stays hidden when I have company.>>

The lieutenant beside him, Jaz, grinned. Grace had always liked her because she never wasted words. "What kind of cat?"

"A miniature tiger," he said.

"They're beautiful."

"And she knows it." Heron laughed.

Jaz's smile widened as she fingered her braids. "I have a cat named Mozart. I bought him a roll-out piano and make him play it by pointing the laser at the correct key for Mozart's sonatas. I've monetized it."

Heron returned her smile. "What an entrepreneurial spirit you have, Lieutenant."

She seemed pleased by this praise. She turned away when someone called her name.

Grace, meanwhile, shifted the package nervously against her chest. What if Heron was right? What if it didn't work? What if Dr. Cyrah refused to corroborate their evidence? Or what if the reaction she hoped for didn't play out? Then what would she do?

You'll figure it out, Gray.

Davion's bright, reassuring smile accompanied the bittersweet memory. His large hand on her shoulders, squeezing before pulling her against him.

You can do this.

She didn't know if this was true, but she knew she had to try. What did she have to lose?

The vehicle dropped them off at the upper level of the precinct building. They took the elevator down, most still awash in the excitement of the raid. But Heron was silent beside her, and he stayed that way when she stepped off the elevator and went straight to Dr. Cyrah's holding chamber. The wall had been turned to a view of the opposite park where three large crows picked at the artificial grass.

"Well?" she said.

"Your boss is dead," Grace said by way of introduction. "He plunged a syringe into his throat rather than face the repercussions of his actions."

Dr. Cyrah was stricken. Her face elongated as her jaw fell open. "Getty is dead?"

"When we told him that we knew about the deleted employees, and the fact that he'd unlawfully expunged their identities and citizenship in order to prevent paying their wages and tax—I guess he wasn't interested in seeing it through to the end."

"I don't know what you're talking about," she said.

"Oh, don't be like that," Heron pouted. He turned a chair around and straddled it so that he could look directly into the doctor's eyes. "We're here to help *you* help *us*."

Dr. Cyrah, curled up on her sofa bed, looked rightfully suspicious.

"We want to offer you a plea bargain," Grace said. "It would lessen the severity of your sentence in exchange for helping us. I'm sure you'd rather *not* ride the Midnight Train."

"I killed Ravee," she said, tears in her eyes. "I can't take that back."

Grace wasn't sure if this was real remorse—which often developed with prolonged periods in solitary containment cells—or if she only felt sorry for herself. It didn't matter.

"No, you can't," Grace said gently. "But you can give a thousand other people back their lives. One thousand lives restored for the one you took."

She looked down at her hands, and tears fell onto her knuckles, shining against her skin. She smeared it with a swipe of her thumb.

When she lifted her head, Grace saw the fire in those eyes.

"Tell me what to do."

GRACE STOOD AT THE EDGE OF THE STAGE AND TOOK A deep breath. She adjusted the portrait under her arm nervously.

"You'll do great," Heron said. He stood just offstage, hands in his pockets. It reminded her of being on this stage with her husband and son, the night she was made Commander. Had it really only been two years ago? And how much had changed since then . . . she was terrified to ask where she might be in two more years.

She frowned at him. "Why don't you make the announcement?"

"Me? God, no. I hate public speaking," he said, blustering.

"You're my assistant inspector. You should assist."

"And steal your glory, *Captain, my Captain*? Never."

The red-light cue flashed, and with an earnest push on her back from Heron, Grace stepped out onto the stage. She knew there must be at least two hundred cameras in the room. AI journalists were broadcasting their recordings to the network to be distributed to accordingly, replayed on the daily news. She would hear her own words repeated back to her on the next Informed Citizen report.

You want this, she reminded herself as the mounting panic rose in her throat, threatening to close it. *They must be held accountable.*

This was her voice. Only her own voice, and from now on, it would have to be enough.

Grace cleared her throat and began to speak to the blinking red lights. "Thank you for coming. I'm Commander Grace Buteo of the Zone 2 Precinct. Earlier this week, we were requested to investigate a theft at the medical plant known as Viscosity Incorporated here in Zone 2. During the course of the investigation, we uncovered some horrific and devastating practices that Viscosity consumers, as well as the citizens of Zone 2, should now be made aware of."

<<There you go,>> Heron pinged. <<They'll definitely reelect you if you keep this up.>>

<<Do not make me smile,>> she warned. <<It will make me seem heartless.>>

As if her scarred face wasn't already disturbing enough.

Obediently, Heron remained silent for the remainder of her announcement.

"Our investigation led us to believe that Viscosity Inc.

knowingly and willingly deleted citizen files and identities from the network server in order to avoid paying those citizens' wages, living expenses, and accrued ecological taxes. All businesses who are given permits in Zone 2 agree to these stipulations in exchange for a tax-free business license in our zone. This means they may hire and recruit talent from any zone but must bear the burden of that citizen's livelihood and compensate for the ecological expenses the employee and their family incur. It is now clear that Viscosity did not comply with these requirements and violated several of the resource-management policies required by Zone 2 law. Viscosity must be held accountable for its fraud and human rights violations. If there are other companies in our zone utilizing the same unlawful practices, they will face the same consequences."

The AIs continued to blink red lights at her. One with a placid, emotionless face asked, "Why would any company do this?"

"To expand their bottom line at the expense of the lives they destroyed."

"What proof do you have?" another blank face asked.

"We have a senior official from the company and several former employees who are willing to testify against Viscosity. We also have physical evidence to corroborate their statements."

Grace held up the confiscated photo now for the media to see.

<<Good, let them get a good long look and record it,>> Heron encouraged. <<It will be harder for those scoundrels to cover up their tracks if we have a thousand recordings of it bouncing around the network.>>

"This is a group photo of Viscosity employees from lab fourteen. In it, you will see two men, Sam Crate and Tomas Lake." She pointed to each in turn, angling the photo to make sure all of the recording and broadcasting AI's could see the men and compare it against their interior logs. "You will find that no matter how hard you search the network directory files, you cannot identify these men. That is because Viscosity *deleted* them."

"You cannot prove that."

"I can," Grace insisted. "All of the other employees save one are willing to testify that they know and can vouch for the two men in the photograph, that they were employees of the company before disappearing."

"It could be a manipulated photograph in order to destroy a good company's name," another AI suggested. "These men may not even exist."

"I assure you that these men are real and they are victims." She looked offstage. "Please, allow me to introduce Dr. Sam Crate."

Grace swept her hand toward the side stage as Sam stepped out into the light.

TWENTY-ONE

GRACE STOOD in the precinct and watched the news reports come in. Getty Peters was found posthumously guilty of fraud, crimes against humanity, and a dozen lesser violations. The company's worth plummeted instantly. It seemed no one wanted to purchase organs from a company with a reputation for exploiting its people.

Praise persisted in the precinct itself. While it wasn't quite as terrible as before, it was still incredibly uncomfortable for Grace.

"She's done it again. She's on a roll!"

"Commander, really, it's unbelievable. How do you seem to know?"

"Because she's our very own Goddess of Justice."

She bore all this ridiculousness the best she could, but the muscles in her face, especially the ruined side, had taken to twitching in protest at their overuse.

Heron pinged her. <<Take a breath, Grace. You look like you're sucking a lemon. We're celebrating here.>>

She turned away from the television overhead to find him leaning against a wall, talking to a handsome young cop. Adams stepped into her view before she could muster a smile.

As soon as she saw him, the small object in her pocket grew heavy. She'd carried it since taking it from Peters's office, as if by holding it, she could make sense of it.

He shuffled toward her through the gathered crowd still watching the news break.

"Leave some heroics for the rest of us, will you, Buteo?" Adams said. He was smiling. "Every time I turn around, you're saving the day."

"It's my job," Grace said, crossing her arms over her chest.

She waited. She knew Adams well enough to know that he wasn't here to congratulate her on doing her job.

"Two things," he said, organizing his thoughts before sharing them. It was a compulsion that Grace found amusing. "One, I don't know if you noticed, but—"

"Commander Hank Roger is back." Her statue had been replaced with its original, and a belt had been loosened from her chest when she'd seen it arrive this morning. "So where was I moved to?"

"You're in Eastside," he said. "In the Plaza Cortona."

"Good," she said. "I never go to Plaza Cortona."

He sighed.

"The second thing?" she prompted.

"Your request to speak to Richards privately was denied."

Her heart skipped a beat. "Denied?"

"Judge Moracant seems to think it . . . unwise. You can still speak to him, as his last rights demand, but it will have to be supervised."

<<Interesting,>> Heron pinged. Grace refrained from looking at him and giving away their conversation. <<And somewhat telling, isn't it?>>

"I'm sorry," Adams was saying.

"It wasn't essential," Grace said, as if her heart wasn't clogging her throat and pounding out a terrible rhythm in her temples.

I should've asked for the other one. That's what Peters had said.

She thought of Adams on her first day back, which now seemed like ages ago. *Getty Peters requested you.*

I should've asked for the other one.

The other one. The only other one was Adams himself. Her co-commander and friend.

Are you part of the problem? she wondered. *Am I going to have to watch my back against you too?*

Adams seemed disturbed by her questioning silence, by her intense glare. He licked his lips and began again, hesitantly. "I know you wanted closure, but we don't always get that. Life is messy." He shook his head as if realizing what he was saying and who he was saying it to. "As you well know."

Grace slipped her hand into her pocket and clasped the object hidden there. The evidence she took from Getty Peters's desk.

Don't, she thought. *Don't show him because if you do, he'll know you know.*

"Grace, I've wanted to—" Adams began.

"Shhh," she told him, her hand releasing the object in her pocket. She stepped closer to the television. "This is the part I've been waiting for."

Seeing her interest, Lore Duchovny turned up the volume on the screen.

"Viscosity rival Plasticity has agreed to rehire more than eight hundred of the company's employees in light of the recent findings, including whistle-blower Sam Crate, who is believed to have helped uncover the Machiavellian corruption eroding Viscosity from the inside out. Other local medical groups, including Mercy General, Habsworth Dentistry, and Yorkshire Cryogenics, have also reached out and offered jobs to former employees."

Heron barged into her head again. He was getting far too comfortable in there. << No one wants to look like the bad guy. I'd bet a boyfriend that many of those companies hired back their own ghosts with signature nondisclosure requirements and hefty bonuses. Then they took on a few more for publicity's sake.>>

Grace had to agree with Heron on that one. She knew this was a financially calculated move. The corporations were not their friends. Social justice messages from corporations were almost always self-serving. They wanted to snap up the business Viscosity was hemorrhaging, improve their own public images, and save themselves from the same fate.

<<Bet a boyfriend?>> she asked. <<You have one to spare?>>

This earned her a devilish smile.

The report droned on. "Plasticity, a company focused on the creation and storage of organs, plasma, and other bio products, has certainly seen public support for the move. Their stock value has jumped sixty-one percent since the announcement."

<<I suspect most of the victims will accept these jobs just to secure their place in Zone 2,>> Heron pinged.

She agreed. They might choose a new company, a new offer. But most of them will take the offer. <<Let's hope none of the companies are stupid enough to make the same mistake. If they are—>>

<<What about the others who are still underground? >>

She'd been thinking about them too. "We'll take care of it," she said aloud.

"Excuse me?" Commander Adams said. He thought Grace was speaking to him.

She turned and faced him. "This investigation isn't closed. The Viscosity theft case is wrapped up, but they weren't the only company who threw their employees out on the streets. I'm going to introduce legislation that requires quarterly reports and public employee records. Anything to make it impossible for employees to simply *disappear*."

Adams shifted uncomfortably. "You have no proof any other companies were doing the same thing."

"I will," she said with a challenging smile. "Give me time."

The other one would do what he's told.

"Unless you plan to intervene?" she asked.

Adams frowned. "Why would I interfere in your work, Commander?"

"I don't know," Grace said, not pretending to smile.

Sam Crate stepped into the precinct with his wife and daughter in tow. Grace waved the smiling man over and braced herself for the painful relief of seeing another family restored.

To Adams she said, "Why would you?"

TWENTY-TWO

THEY TOOK Heron's unmarked auto back to the city of ghosts under cover of nightfall. Heron's auto appeared to make itself all but invisible on the quiet streets as it rolled into the tight space between the two shipping complexes and cloaked itself.

"Truly," she asked him once they were inside and their voices could be swallowed by the never-ending darkness in their descent. "Do you spend all of your money on gadgets?"

"No, I play with forty percent at most," he said. There was a slight tremor in his voice. She could tell he was nervous about tonight, about meeting her in the bar to have their discussion, after they finished this last piece of business for the day. "Another thirty percent goes to Arjun. He isn't cheap, you know."

Her expression drew a laugh from Heron.

"I don't mind," he said. "I like a man who knows his worth. A woman, too."

She could only focus on closing her mouth.

It was Tomas who greeted them at the entrance,

ushering them into the underground before they could be seen. With a silent command, Heron sent his car away.

The City of Ghosts was quite different now. At first, she thought it was the time. Maybe most of the people were at dinner or settling down for the evening with their families. She quickly realized that wasn't it.

"Most have gone up. Everyone with children, but most of the old and young too. It seemed only the truly idealistic wanted to stay," Tomas informed her. He pointed his thumb to the sky. "Most took jobs at different companies, hoping for a better outcome this time. They also insisted on ironclad contracts. We advised everyone to use your law firm, and most of them have."

Grace turned to Heron, confused.

<<Just giving them a bit of free legal advice. Something else to tell you about over drinks tonight.>>

"That's great," Grace said aloud, turning back to Tomas. "They deserve to have the lives promised to them."

"What about the ones still here?" Heron asked.

Tomas shook his head. "Many are skeptical. They don't want to be dependent on corporations they don't trust. I agree that a corporation shouldn't be able to make or break you. Most of those who've stayed behind came from mediocre zones. They've known moderate security all their lives. Those who came from truly impoverished zones were the first to go up. They knew what they had to lose."

"Of course they did," Heron agreed, sliding his hands in his pockets.

"But I think more will go up," Tomas said. "The underground isn't the same with so many gone. It seems . . ."

"Sad," Grace offered.

Tomas looked surprised, but he nodded. "Yes. It's not like we *wanted* to be down here, worrying every day about keeping everyone fed and safe. But we had each other. There was something special about it."

"What will you do now?" Heron asked.

"I accepted a position at Plasticity," he said. "I moved my family back upside, but I spend a lot of time down here making sure everyone is okay."

"How many are left?"

"About two hundred," he said. "That's why most of the medical professionals who moved upside are still coming back down. Who else is going to run the med tables?"

"I won't force you to go up," Grace said. "But if you're caught here—"

Tomas smiled. "They know the risk. That isn't why I called you here today."

Heron and Tomas exchanged looks.

"What?" she asked, her pulse quickening.

Tomas licked his lips nervously. "You asked me if I knew your husband. Davion."

The world tilted beneath her.

Tomas didn't seem to notice. "I knew *of* him. He was one of the first people to help us."

"Help you how?" she blurted.

"He set up the programming that allowed us to steal from the shipments without being detected. He had the med tables delivered to a nonexistent address. Food rerouted. But you need to know something else."

"More than my husband illegally programming the network?" she whispered. Her constricting throat wouldn't allow her to say more.

Tomas seemed not to hear. "Lix was one of us." He finally met her eyes. "He was fired from Mercy General and deleted, and he came to live with us here after Crate found him wandering around Whitman Park. Your husband and Lix knew each other."

Her heart thrummed so loudly in her ears it sounded like high winds. The belt had returned, tightening her chest to the point where only small breaths were possible.

Run CALM program?

"No," she said.

"We don't believe Lix would hurt your husband. He was helping us. But the only way to know for sure is to speak to him."

"Lix is in a containment cell. He'll be put on the Midnight Train in two days," Grace said.

"I still might be able to help you." Tomas waved them forward, guiding them through the lanterned city. "One of our programs is an off-network communication server."

"How in the world—" she began.

"Necessity is the mother of invention," Tomas said. "We couldn't use the network to communicate once we'd been expunged, so we had to make a new one. Your husband helped us work out the early bugs. But we can only use it to talk to each other."

He sounded almost like he was trying to prove to her that he had a reason to need this software.

Because I'm still the law, she thought. *He sees me on the other side of the line. Like I might take it away.*

"Lix could still be on this network." He led them to metal stairs leaning against the mouth of a shipping container. He began to climb, calling down after her, "Inspector Jane said you needed to speak with him."

"I do," she said, perhaps too quickly. "If that's possible."

Heron clapped his hands together. "Wait until you see the terminal."

"Terminal?" she asked, following Tomas up the ladder.

"It's a relic," Heron said. He sounded excited and not at all lost down here in the dark. That was when Grace knew that he'd been back in the two weeks since they'd wrapped up the case. Probably more than once.

<<I hope all of this is part of your story,>> she pinged him.

<<It is,>> he assured her. <<Just a few more hours, Grace. Hold on.>>

They stepped into the second-level shipping container, which smelled of rust and dust. Tomas turned on a lantern. Soft light flooded the space. Two terminals were set up against one wall with a chair in front of them. The external screen—god, when was the last time she'd seen one?—glowed green.

Heron fell into the seat with a giddy squeal of delight. "I hadn't seen one of these since I did a summer with my mother in the field. I was ten. That was almost thirty years ago."

"What is it?"

"A port," he said. "Scientists like my mother use them for data storage and collection and other computations when a network isn't available. Everything goes in and can be retrieved later."

"We were using it to aggregate our messages," Tomas said. "It means that communication is delayed by fifteen seconds between messages, but everything goes through. It's impressive when you think about how completely removed from the network it is."

"Barbaric lag times," Heron said, tapping out a tune on the table. "But a small price to pay for a message that isn't on the network. I think my encrypted messages have a zero-point-zero-zero-three-second delay."

When they only looked at him, Heron added, "Ninety percent of my messages are sent on a private encrypted server."

"Still, a zero-point-zero-zero-three-second delay is pretty good. What do you use to boost it?"

Heron held up his finger with the dark ring on it.

"Nice," Tomas said, nodding appreciatively.

"So about Richards," Grace interjected. "You can still contact him, even though he's detained?"

"It's possible, since the server was private. They would have disrupted his network connection when they arrested him, but this isn't on the network," he said. "This is cloned software."

"Will they know I contacted him?

Tomas threw up his hands. "Honestly, I don't know. I've never tried to contact someone in custody. We need to mask your profile to be safe, before we connect you to the terminal. Then you'll have to deal with the delay."

"I'll try to speed it up a bit," Heron said. "But I suspect we'll have to wait."

Heron's fingers flew over the tabletop.

"Aren't you worried someone might see you?" Grace asked. It didn't seem he'd taken any time to erect safety measures of his own.

"My server is cloaked. If someone comes looking, I'll be alerted, and they'll have a hell of a time getting past my firewall."

Grace settled into the chair and tried to compose herself. Lix Richards. What would she even say?

Did you do it? That would be the first question, of course. But after that . . .

"You know," Heron said, glancing at the silent Tomas, who leaned against the wall. "If Davion was helping you, do you think someone was onto him?"

"It's possible," Tomas said as he continued typing on the terminal. "He did a lot in the zone, not just for us. Not just operations down here but also visas."

"Anything worth killing him over?" Heron asked.

"Cybercrime convictions are pretty severe. But usually arrest is the first step, isn't it?" Tomas asked.

They were looking to her for an answer, but her mind was reeling. She didn't know what to say.

Davion, Davion, what did you do?

Heron leaned toward Grace. "Can I touch the back of your neck? I need to put this booster over your router. I want to make sure you're masked and getting optimal speed."

Grace lifted her hair so the patch of flesh behind her left ear was accessible. Heron removed the cuff from his left ear and hooked it over her helix. It was still warm with his body heat.

"Do you know that all disposables used to be made of plastic?" he said into her ear. His breath was hot against the side of her face. "Now we use all recyclable plant fibers and silicones."

"How much easier it would've been to survive with those heaps of trash around," Tomas said. "We would've had an excellent selection, wouldn't we? What a city we could've built."

Heron snorted. "I don't think that city would've been so grand."

The blue light lit on the left side of Grace's head, and she saw a chat box open on her lenscape.

"You'll have to talk first," Heron said, his fingers tapping on the desktop.

<<Lix?>> she asked. <<Lix Richards?>>

He didn't immediately ping back. Instead, the message hung on her lenscape, the question mark seemingly more pronounced by this pause. It was seventeen seconds before words appeared.

<<Who is this?>> came the unmarked reply.

That's when she realized that her handle had also been removed from the conversation.

She hesitated.

"What's wrong?" Heron whispered, as if Richards might overhear them.

"Should I tell him my name?" she asked.

"You're probably safe," Heron said. "I don't see anything on this channel and I'm sweeping it constantly."

What choice did she have? How could she ask the questions she wanted to ask and say the things she wanted to say if she remained anonymous?

<<This is Grace Buteo. I was denied the option of seeing you in real time, so I've resorted to other means. I'm contacting you this way with the help of mutual friends.>>

Again, her words hung in the lenscape, amplified by the black space and nonresponse.

<<Did you do it?>> she asked. She found she couldn't wait any longer. She couldn't hold it inside her even if she wanted to. <<Did you kill my husband and son?>>

And then, <<How could you?>>

And then, <<Why?>>

Tears stung her eyes.

"Are you—" Tomas began.

"Shhh." Heron cut him off with a raised hand.

<<I'm so sorry, Grace.>>

Her heart hammered, beating out its furious rhythm.

<<I didn't kill them.>>

Her stomach dropped.

<<I was there at the precinct the night the bomb went off. I came to the precinct to speak to Davion. He wanted to introduce us, you and me. I was close, waiting for the cue. But before he gave it, you went inside the precinct. Then everyone was running, and it all went to hell. I was arrested and brought to detention before I even under-

stood what was going on. I didn't know he was dead until the trial.>>

Grace's mind reeled, trying to take all of this in.

Lix, unaware of her overwhelm, carried on. <<I've received no formal review, no offer of attorney. If they'd asked for them, I could've shown all of my minutes from that day. I can prove I never entered that precinct. I came to talk to you. I came to ask for your help because Davion said it was time.>>

Her heart was beating so fast that it felt like it was levitating in her chest, rising until it clogged the bottom of her throat.

No trial? No questioning? No formal review?

Why wouldn't they offer him these things? Even if he was in the zone unauthorized and found to be guilty of a crime, he was guaranteed the right to provide evidence of his innocence. Innocent until proven guilty. The only way all of his basic rights had been overlooked is . . . if someone—*someones*—would've had to knowingly block justice at every turn.

No, she thought. *No, no, no.*

She didn't want to believe she'd lost everything for a city so corrupt.

<<Prove it,>> she replied.

And he did by sending her a cache file of the last day of his free life.

TWENTY-THREE

GRACE ENTERED the bar and waited for the AI to confirm her age. Even before she passed the security checkpoint, she saw Heron in a booth, six rows back. He was talking into the neck of his beer bottle. Arjun had his arm slung over Heron's shoulder.

Arjun seemed to sense her enter the bar, because he looked up and met her gaze first. Then he smiled. Grace didn't like the way it was forced into the corners of his mouth. It made something in her tighten.

Arjun leaned over and spoke into Heron's ear. Both men looked up.

Heron's smile was even weaker, but he waved her over.

He looks like he's boarding the Midnight Train, she thought.

How bad must it be? Whatever confession he was about to make . . .

Before Grace reached the booth, slowed by the thick crowd of jovial bodies, Arjun stood. He bent and kissed Heron briefly. Grace thought she read *good luck* on his lips, but then he was walking in the opposite direction, toward the back of the bar and its rear exit.

"He didn't have to leave," Grace said by way of hello. Resting one hand on the tabletop, she slid into the booth. "This isn't work related."

"He was just keeping me company until you got here," Heron said, bringing the bottle to his lips again. "I don't like to sit in these places alone. People always come up and talk to me, which is fine if they're interesting, but usually they aren't. It's the ones who *think* they're interesting who introduce themselves. Absolutely horrible."

The menu screen lit up in front of her. It was triggered by either her weight on the seat or the movement of her hand across the tabletop.

"Does his job bother you?" She wasn't sure how to begin this conversation.

"No. Yes." Heron shrugged. "Loyalty and love aren't about genitals, Grace."

She cringed at the word *genitals*. Sure there was another way to say it. "How long have you been together?"

"Officially? Eight years," he said.

"So he moved here with you?"

"He did. But he wanted his own place for obvious reasons. So I pay double the rent."

She considered ordering a glass of dry red wine from the menu. She felt nervous. Her limbs trembled with extra energy and her chest felt compressed as if readying itself for a blow. Her mind screamed, *Tell me everything!* Calmly she said, "What are you drinking?"

"This? Oh, this is a lovely little local craft. It's got a GreenScore of ten because they grow all the ingredients in this zone. The oats, long-rye, and goberries."

He offered her the bottle across the tabletop, and she took it. She pressed her lips to the glass. The ring was warm from his mouth, the bottle itself frosty under her fingertips.

"It's too sweet," she said and slid it back. She ordered her red wine.

"It's the goberries. Did you know . . ." He began in a way that eased her. She leaned into the booth, her shoulders relaxing. ". . . when the strawberries, blueberries, and blackberries all started dying out, they used modification to try and create a berry that would survive the changing climate? Something that required a lot less water and could thrive in drier, clay-based soils. That's how the goberry was born. It's how most of our modern plants evolved, actually. We ran the lands fallow, polluted the water sources, and then had to make food that would survive in our mess."

She sighed and accepted the glass of red wine from the opening receiving box. "I feel like there's a metaphor in there somewhere."

"Maybe." He shrugged. He seemed to consider the possibility seriously. "Life goes on."

"Life goes on," she repeated and took another sip. "Until it doesn't."

"Even if we managed to kill our species, something would go on, wouldn't it? So yes, that's the message: life goes on. But not for Lix Richards."

She drank her first glass too fast and ordered a second. Heron's melancholy mood was contagious.

"I'm told he was found dead without any sign of struggle," Heron said, finishing off his beer and ordering another. "Funny, considering we spoke to him three hours ago."

"They moved him to the general population section of detainment two hours after we spoke to him and then one hour later he was dead," she said.

"Wonder why." There was absolutely *zero* curiosity in Heron's voice.

"If they'd found a young, healthy man with no sign of

malice dead in his solitary containment cell, that would have pointed fingers at the people in charge. This way they can blame it on the other inmates. Or at least throw enough doubt to protect themselves."

"The real question is whether they were already planning to kill him. Or if they killed him because they know he talked to us."

She turned the wineglass in the light, watching the liquid sparkle.

"Do you think it was my call that killed him?" she asked. Her throat was unbearably tight.

"Grace, you could call me while I was naked in the shower and I could slip and break my neck and be dead, and would you say it was your fault?"

She nodded but wasn't sure why.

"Did someone think he talked and got nervous? It's possible. But they killed him to protect themselves. It's not like you drove a knife into his throat."

"The only people who could get to him are *our* people," she said. "You realize that, right? And they didn't offer him a lawyer or formal review. I checked the record and it said he refused both, but he didn't. Someone *framed* him. And now I can't even fight for him."

"That's not on you either," Heron said. His cheeks were pink.

"It's probably someone we know," she said. Adams? *I should've requested the other one.*

How deep was the corruption? Was she the *only* good cop left in Zone 2? She hoped not. She *really* hoped not.

"Maybe that's all crime is." Heron seemed unaware of her crisis. "People using whatever means they can to meet their needs, which would have been met if the system delivered on its promises."

"Maybe you see more than I do," she said. "Davion

used to say I have tunnel vision. He said that when I was on a hunt, the rest of the world fell away."

"What else did Davion say?" Heron asked cautiously.

Grace laughed. A short, high, almost panicked sound. "I don't know. I've been replaying every conversation we ever had, and I just don't know. Sometimes I think he was trying to tell me something important."

She finished the second glass of red wine and ordered a third.

"And now?" he asked. "What do you think?"

Now.

What did that word even mean to her?

It was so hard for her to stay here *now*. In this moment, in this place. She didn't just mean this bar. No matter how hard she tried, she kept going backward in time. Back to when she was a mother. When she was a wife.

She was none of those things *now*.

"I think...I've been getting out of bed every morning just to spite myself," she said finally. "My anger. My self-disgust was enough to get me up and moving. I blamed myself for getting them killed. Sometimes, it was because I should've been in the auto. Other times, it was because we should've been at home. I didn't want to go to the parade. I was tired. I should've kept us home. Blaming me—it's easier. It's easier than this...than this idea that Davion is to blame."

Heron picked at the bottle's label with his thumb. "I have something to tell you, Grace. Thank you for being patient enough to wait, because I've been terrified. I won't lie about that. And I have to tell you the truth before we go any further with...with any of this."

"Is that why you sent Arjun away?"

"Yes," he said without hesitation. He smiled. "I'll need him to rescue me if this goes badly."

"If you're afraid of how I'll react, why tell me at all?" she asked.

Heron made a short, sharp laugh. His face seemed to say, *Why indeed?* "I made a promise to an old friend. I keep my promises."

"You'd better spit it out then," she said, her heart racing. She felt her pulse in her temples. "Before you scare me into overreacting."

"I wonder if we should do this back at your place, instead of publicly."

She arched an eyebrow. "Do *what?*"

He kept picking at the bottle's label with his thumb, tearing away a strip of paper. "Maybe we'll start with the truth here, and if you can stomach it without arresting me, I'll ask you where you want to hear the rest."

He wasn't speaking to her. He was puzzling it out himself.

Watching his serious contemplation made her heartbeat throb even harder. "Please just tell me. You're killing me with the setup."

He licked his lips. He searched her face as if looking for a seam, a door, a way to enter this conversation. "I'm not a police inspector. I've had no formal training. I used technology to craft my identity and forged an occupational visa. I won't be caught for it unless you turn me in. I'm very good at altering records. In fact, I learned from the best."

Her pulse moved into her ears.

"I learned from the man I roomed with at university. He didn't have money for all his books or even half his meals, and I was a shit programmer. We made a good team. Of course, he graduated brilliantly and was offered an amazing job in Zone 2. I went home to skulk in my mothers' mansion and play in her many businesses, including the law firm Lake mentioned. She established it for environmental law, actually—never mind. That doesn't matter."

He took a long drink of his beer. Grace tried to force air into her lungs.

"I first met your husband when he was a boy in the outlands. My mother was researching a declining bird population by looking at its migration path. We became friends. My mother seemed delighted that I was finally starting to care about poverty and the plight of the world. She's a do-gooder, if you didn't know, so imagine how hard it was for her to raise a selfish son. Then it was time for me to go back home and I wanted to keep in touch with the strange little boy from nowhere. And we did. We stayed friends all the way to university, and during those four years as well. We spent a lot of time together in school. After graduation, it went back to how it was when we were kids. We sent each other updates on our lives apart. He told me about his new job. He told me about meeting an amazing, smart woman with a steel spine."

"No," she whispered.

Heron, even if he'd heard, kept speaking. "He told me about the birth of his son, and that he'd graduated from helping spoiled rich brats through university to falsifying visas. He was using his power and gifts not just to help good kids get into schools in better zones. He was moving entire families from the worst zones into safer ones. He worried that someone was onto him. Someone in his wife's own precinct. And he made me promise—"

"No," she said again, a little louder. "*No.*"

"—promise that if anything happened to him, I would come here. To Zone 2. That I'd give his wife a message and help her any way I could because if he was caught, it was only a matter of time before they got to her, too."

She couldn't get enough air into her lungs. Something was wrong with her chest. It wouldn't expand.

"When I heard Davion had died, I searched for this *wife*. I found out that there was an opening in her own department, and I altered the application so that only I could apply. Of course, I forged all the details and background necessary to make myself suitable enough to pass an interview, and here I am."

"He knew someone was onto him," she said, searching Heron's face.

"Yes," he said. "He knew his life was in danger and wanted to make sure you—"

"Me," she hissed, slamming a fist against the table. Both the wineglass and beer bottle jumped. "*Me*! What about our *son*? What about our *fucking* son?"

Heron pressed his lips together, his own eyes bright with unshed tears.

"Didn't he even consider, for a *moment*, that maybe poking around where he *shouldn't*, doing what he *shouldn't*, would have an effect on *Kaiden*? Did he think about him for a *second*?"

A pair in the opposite booth looked her way nervously. She realized she was too loud. She lowered her voice.

"*Did* he?" she hissed between clenched teeth, gripping the edge of the table so hard that the wine in her glass trembled and her fingers paled, bloodless. "*Did* he?"

Heron took another sip. "No. I don't think he did."

"For fuck's sake," she moaned, covering her face with her hands.

"There's more."

She waved him on.

Run the CALM program?

Grace muted her lenscape.

"So I arrive in the precinct, and I pass the interview.

The first day on the job, I meet my friend's wife. She's everything he said she was and more. She's fierce, she's smart, she's got a brilliant eye for detail, and she knows almost immediately that I'm not who I say I am."

Grace tried to follow the sound of Heron's voice but it was hard. Too hard.

She pushed against all the images of Kaiden flooding her mind. Sweet flashes of a dimpled smile. Of his arms outstretched. Kaiden as a baby. Kaiden as she held him for the first time. Kaiden as he toddled toward her, arms outstretched.

Damn you, Davion. Damn you.

Heron carried on unaware of how completely she was unravelling. "We start working our first case and it's clear from the start something is going on. I realize pretty quickly that Lake and Crate have been deleted from the system, and—knowing what Davion told me—I wonder if these were the people he was helping. I invite Lake to my house and I try to convince him to tell you the truth."

"Everything at your house was a setup? By *you*? You were bleeding."

"I took drama in college," he admitted. "Davion did too."

"Oppa seemed pretty—"

"Oh no, not him." Heron shook his head. "He didn't want you to know. That was real. I was worried you suspected. Lake did a fine acting job I thought, but I had to give him that little tête-à- tête in the bedroom before the second act."

All of it. All of it was lies. For years, probably. Her marriage, certainly. Maybe even her whole life.

"I wanted you to know the truth, but I was afraid of what you might do with it."

Heron fell silent. He watched her. He waited. "Grace?"

For a long time, she couldn't speak. She also couldn't get up and leave. She thought about it. She saw herself rise and exit the bar without so much as a word to Heron.

Finally she said, "Why does everyone lie to me, Heron? You. My own husband. People I work with. Everyone lies."

"You have a lot of power, Grace. It scares people. They can't be sure what you'll do with it."

"I just want to know everything. Is that too much to ask?" she whispered.

Heron arched a brow. "If you want to know everything, then I should tell you there's more."

Instinctively, she braced herself. "More? There's *more*?"

"There's a video that he sent explaining it all," he said. "I can share it via the lenscape unless you want to watch it in private."

"Have you already seen it?" Grace asked.

"Yes," he said.

"Then show me," she said, sitting up straighter in the booth. The muscles in her ruined cheek were twitching.

"Are you sur—"

"*Show* me," she said, punching each word between her lips.

<<Accept private chat with heronjane1?>>

Her lenscape filled with the image of her husband, sitting in the booth where Heron now sat. She could still see his blue eyes shining through, like two faces laid on top of one another, and she adjusted the transparency in her scape so that her husband was as tangible as the memories she played to help her sleep at night.

Gray, he said clearly over the roar of the bar, speaking as if his lips were against her ear. *I never wanted to make a video like this, but I think I have to. Something just happened.*

He looked down at his lap. *Let me start over.*

He seemed to search her face for a moment, as if she

were really there, listening to him, waiting for him to articulate his last missives.

The stories you've been told about the outer zones are lies, he
said. *I didn't even realize how much manipulation and propaganda
there was until I tried to contact my family a couple of years ago.
The picture my mother and brother painted—food shortages, starvation, pollution—you can't imagine it. If Heron has given you this
message, then they caught me. I will never see trial because they would
never want me to tell the truth on public record. I'll probably be
mysteriously killed or I'll disappear. Maybe I will have an accident at
work or . . . I don't know. But I can't bear the idea that you might
think I left you, so I have to tell you all of this now, before anything
happens. You're going to be pissed. God, you're going to be out-of-
your-mind pissed at me, but just in case they move quickly, I want to
make sure this gets to you. So please, just listen, even if you are angry
with me.*

You have no idea, she thought.

*I've been overriding the network's immigration algorithms. Right
now they are programmed to only offer placement to the most profitable
citizens, those most likely to improve the wealth and prosperity of a
zone, or improve its public image. Instead, I've manipulated those
ratings so I can transfer families from the roughest zones into more
stable ones. I showed Heron how to do this for himself so he could
deliver this message to you. He can also use it again if you and
Kaiden need to leave Zone 2. He will tell you anything you want to
know about the work I've done for the families, what strategies I used,
everything. But I don't have time to explain that now.*

He seemed to realize he was wandering.

*I've moved three hundred and sixty-seven families. Most of them
had children. So many were Kaiden's age or younger because I had
such a hard time turning those away. I can only hope relocating them
was enough to give them a chance at a good life. I would have saved a
million families if I could, but today—after today—I have to stop.
At least for a while.*

He licked his lips and looked directly into the camera. Directly into Grace's eyes.

Today I found out that one of the families I tried to place in Zone 6 was taken into custody. After hours of torture, the woman gave up as much information about me as she could to prevent her remaining two children from being killed. It's my understanding that at least one of her children was murdered, which is why she gave up what she had on me. I don't blame her, but it does put us at great risk. I'm already fabricating new identities, covering all my tracks. I'm going to start using a new code that I designed. It's basically self-destructing, unraveling behind me after I use it. It was only in beta, but it'll have to do. Hopefully it will better mask my operations when I'm ready to start up again.

"This can't be what he was killed for," she whispered. A whole city was living beneath their own and no one bothered to raise a fuss.

"Keep watching," Heron said.

You have to understand that I had to fund the relocation expenses for these families, Davion said, staring into the camera with urgent desperation. *Some of them are traveling through forty or fifty zones in a matter of days. It's not a quick or cheap journey to get them here, let alone secure their housing, their paperwork, and so on. And that money had to come from somewhere.*

"You didn't," she whispered.

I took only from the wealthiest corporations, places where I felt like the missing money wouldn't be noticed, he said.

She put her head in her hands and groaned. "Davion."

When I pulled money from Trinity Trust, I realized I made a mistake. There was a tracker embedded in the funds I lifted. It had burrowed quite deep before I found and isolated the spyder. If that's the end of it, then we're fine. But the truth is, I have no idea how much information it was able to retrieve about me before I caught it.

"How did you think that could be the end of it?" she hissed.

"Watch your voice," Heron cautioned, bringing his beer to his lips again, but his eyes swept the bar.

If it was transmitting data, it's entirely possible they know who I am now. That's why I'm sending this message to Heron with my instructions. It hasn't even been twenty minutes since I found the tracker, but I would rather be safe than sorry. It's impossible to know how quickly they'll act.

He looked down at his hands.

I'm not ashamed of what I did, he told her. *I can't live my life enjoying all that I have and not try to help other people who are suffering. But I do have one regret.*

Her throat tightened.

I'm sorry that I didn't tell you sooner. I think I was afraid you'd ask me to stop. That you would make me choose between Kaiden and the other children.

"Yes. Yes, I would have."

And I knew I wouldn't be able to do that. I hope you can forgive me. You help so many people in your job. I wanted to do the same.

He ran a hand over his face. *Either way, I'm telling you the truth tonight. I think I've figured out how to do it. I'll bring someone to the parade. Hopefully his story will help you see the truth about this zone—and what they're doing. There's a whole side to this that you don't see, Gray.*

He looked directly into the camera again.

And I want you to see it.

A small laugh escaped him.

Assuming I make it to the parade, that is. If I don't, if I'm already dead by then, I can only hope that you don't blame me for doing what I felt was right. That you don't regret marrying a man who made a stupid mistake and left you to raise our son alone. I love you, Gray. You're one of the things I'm so grateful for. Both of you. Never doubt that.

The message ended. Her lenscape fell dark to reveal Heron's face once more. He looked as exhausted and stricken as she felt. Tears had filled his eyes and spilled from the corners down his cheeks.

She fell back against the padded seat and steadied her breath. Long, slow inhalations rolled through her until the world came into focus again. Four glasses of wine had made it more than soft around the edges.

Then a memory surfaced, bright and unbearable.

"What?" Heron asked, sitting up straighter.

She couldn't say. She couldn't articulate the emotions rolling her, so she only sent him the request to share her screen, which he accepted in that eerily quick way of his.

Then she replayed the memory.

He's down for the night, Davion said, coming up behind her and slipping his arms around her waist.

I should go in and say goodnight, she said.

And undo all my hard work? Please don't, Davion said. *He'll be too excited to see you to fall back asleep.*

He ran a wide hand over his braided hair and sighed. It would be another six weeks before he would cut it. And oh, how she would miss it when he did.

You make me feel like a terrible mother, she said.

He understands that your job is important.

Your job is important, she'd countered. *You keep this city just as safe, if not safer than I do. What would we do if we didn't have you on the wires?*

His smile tightened. *We're lucky, aren't we?*

Kaiden's lucky, she said and placed a hand on the back of his neck. *He's got you.*

When I think about the kids out there, he said, looking out their moonlit windows, *the ones without water or shelter or anyone to look after them. And they've got no chance whatsoever to build a better life. When I think of them—*

She'd tried to shush him then, the way she had Kaiden when his mind was overrun with thoughts.

It shouldn't just be our child who has what he needs, Davion said, his eyes filled with liquid moonlight. *We need to do more. Grace, I can't live with myself if I don't.*

The memory ended, and Grace found herself in the bar again, looking at Heron across the table.

"How long ago was that?" Heron asked.

"Eight months," she said. "So five months before the accident."

"He was trying to tell you, but he couldn't," Heron said.

"He's been trying to tell me for a long time," she agreed, looking down at her limp hands. Tears fell onto her knuckles, filling the creases like drops of dew. "And what does that say about me?"

"That you have excellent taste in men. He helped over *six hundred* children, Grace."

A knot in her stomach loosened, and in its place she felt . . . pride. She was proud of her husband and loved him even more for his bravery and his courage. But she didn't know if it was enough to forgive him for Kaiden.

Grace would've given back all the children he'd saved if it meant holding Kaiden in her arms again.

All of them. Every single one.

"What do I do with this?" she whispered. She blinked and her tears fell onto the table. "What the *hell* do I do with *this*?"

"First, you decide if you want my help or not," Heron said, turning the bottle between his palms. "I fulfilled my promise to my old friend. I delivered the message. If you don't want me to stick around, I can disappear tomorrow. It's easy enough. I think Adams will be relieved to see me go, actually."

She dragged her hands down her face. "Let's say I can accept that Davion pissed off the wrong person and got killed for it. Would you really stay? You could be killed too."

"I would stay, if you asked me to," he said. And for the first time she saw the pulse jumping in his throat. The skin standing out above his collar.

For some reason, seeing his fear softened her anger.

And there was the terrible truth. She wanted him to stay. She wanted someone—anyone—in this whole zone that she could trust.

For better or worse, she trusted Heron.

She leaned forward in her seat, pointing a finger at him. "I don't want any more secrets. No more wandering around without me. No more side investigations. No more dramas orchestrated to bring me around to the truth. Tell it to me straight or so help me God."

Relief washed over his face. "I can do that."

"And I want to know what you're doing and who you're talking to. At all times. If I have to look for you or, heaven forbid, *save* you, I have to know where the hell to look!"

Heron's lips twitched. "Careful, Gray. I like 'em bossy."

"You tell me *everything*," she said.

"Okay. Well, I can only orgasm if I'm restrained. And I like cheese. And sugar."

"Heron!"

"Hey," he said, hands up. "I'm just saying that I'm fine with no more secrets. More than fine. I'll keep you in the loop."

"You promise?"

"I swear. Does this mean you aren't going to arrest me?" he asked. "For impersonating an officer, for forging a visa, for lying—"

"You were more honest with me than my own husband." And there was a bigger problem. She needed him. If someone was responsible for Davion's death, for

Kaiden's, she would need Heron to help her bring them down.

Their watches beeped at the same time.

"Our toxicity is too high," he said with a lazy smile. "We're well on our way to being drunk, Commander. How do I know that you mean what you say? It could be the booze talking."

Grace laughed. It sounded bitter even to her. "I mean what I say."

"I can really stay on as your assistant inspector? Really? There's no risk to you. If I'm ever caught, you can plead ignorance. It's why I went through all the trouble of making the other one hire me."

The other one would've done as he was told.

And what would Adams do if he knew he'd hired a con man?

"Speaking of Adams," she said, and pulled the gold cylinder from her pocket and put it on the table between them.

Heron's eyes went to the cylinder. "What's that?"

"It's an Egg Island club medal." To her, it looked a little like a scroll.

"Yes, I know about Egg Island. I'm wondering what *you're* doing with it."

"I stole it from Getty's desk," Grace admitted, turning it in the light. The gold surface shimmered.

Heron frowned. "Where have I seen it?"

"There's another one just like it on Adams's desk."

Heron's face slacked with dawning horror. "I'm worried about you, Grace."

He leaned forward conspiratorially.

"It's possible that someone knows what Davion did, and now you've taken down one of the largest corporations in the zone *overnight*. If there is as much corruption here as

I think there is, you're in danger, you know that? *Serious* danger. They will figure out how to get you under control. Or eliminate you."

She wondered why she didn't care more about her own life.

"You can take care of yourself," he said, settling back against the booth. "But there's no shame in accepting my help. Everyone needs someone in their corner."

"You're already *helping*," she said. "You updated my house."

She remembered the red blinking panel the day Heron visited. She hadn't been sure, but now his motives were clear.

His smile twitched. "Caught that, did you? I'm sorry if I overstepped, but your personal security isn't great. I can revert it to the original settings if you prefer. But I'd feel better if you kept the updates."

She couldn't speak. She kept replaying Kaiden's sweet face over and over in her mind.

The urge to conjure up a memory from her bank, replay it, struck her.

Don't, she thought. It was one thing to see him with her mind's eyes. Distant, with a haze of time between them. It would be another to conjure him real and fully fleshed to her present.

You can't. You're not ready, she thought, and knew she was right

Heron seemed unsure of what to do with her silence. "I like working with you. I think we can do a lot of good together. But only if you'll have me."

"There's no shortage of work," she said, finally, slipping the gold cylinder back into her pocket. "But it hurts, Heron. I thought I knew this zone. I can't believe it's rotten from the inside out."

Heron smiled. It was a sad smile. "There's corruption everywhere."

"I suspect sniffing it out will have to be mostly off the books and that we won't necessarily be paid for our—"

"I'm not a man motivated by money." The devilish grin returned, but the sadness had not left his eyes. She could live with that. She was learning to live with a lot. "And I want to stay."

Good, she thought. *Because I want you to stay too.*

She still had enough of her head not to say this aloud. Instead, she said, "What a luxurious life you live if money holds no importance to you. But yes, you should stay."

His face softened, his grin uncontainable.

She threw back the last of her wine. She wouldn't order another. She was done for tonight. She was done for a long time.

"There are worse things to lose," he said. He tilted his head. "You know that."

She wondered if it was a lesson that would ever quit hurting her. Or would she continue to be surprised each time the universe reached out its hand and took something she loved—*someone* she loved—away from her?

"Hey," he said, quietly. The intimacy of his low voice made her look up, pulling her from her thoughts. "It will get better."

"It doesn't feel like it," she said. "It feels like nothing will change. People will keep finding ways to destroy each other and I'll be left here to pick up the pieces."

"No," he said. "No, that's not how it is."

She expected to see doubt flicker through his eyes. Instead, she saw mischievousness. A silent knowing that she wasn't part of. It was enough to spark courage inside her— if only a spark. But maybe that's all she needed to get started.

"Progress isn't a straight line. It doesn't go up and up and up," he said, conceding. "It wobbles all over but it *does* go up."

"How can you be sure?"

"I see you." He reached his hand across the table. "After everything that happened to you, you haven't given up. And you'll never give up. It's that indomitable spirit that will get us through. That's why the world will change. It has to, with people like you around."

She could only look at him. "How can you be sure the world is even capable of change?"

"I'm sure, Grace." He smiled and didn't pull back. He left his hand open, waiting. "I've never been more sure of anything."

TWENTY-FOUR

GRACE STEPPED from the CityRide onto the even walkway encircling the Soul Grove. She removed her shoes, as was customary, and slipped them into an available complimentary cubby, locked by her thumbprint.

She entered the grove. Grass and cool earth pressed into her bare feet. She headed west, toward section C3. Light filtered through the branches above, dancing across her bare arms and face. It was so quiet here. She was sure it was the design acoustics of the grove but also the atmosphere of the place itself. Five rows up, Grace saw a small family. A man and two little girls sat beneath a tree, eating their lunch and speaking quietly.

For a moment, the man looked up and locked eyes with Grace. They shared a sad, knowing smile.

She kept walking until she found who she was looking for.

A basswood tree, still small with its heart-shaped leaves and smooth gray bark, stood silent beside a maple sapling. She'd expected to find the trees and their small video monitors offering the memories of the deceased. What she hadn't counted on was all the offerings.

Flowers and notes. Handmade toys and banners. A shrine of gifts both handmade and purchased.

The zone had shared in her loss. When the auto had lifted off the street and taken the lives of her husband and son—they became more. *The* husband. *The* son. *The* father.

Her heart broke again in that instant, and from the crack emerged a small diamond of hope.

A whispered belief: *There's still good here. There are still people worth protecting.*

Her idyllic zone may not be as much of a paradise as she'd once believed. Someone had framed and killed an innocent man. Someone had taken her husband and son from her. Others had deleted the lives of thousands, exiling them to an underworld. And what other crimes waited to be discovered?

It didn't matter.

Seeing these gifts, seeing the collective heartbreak, reminded her why she *must* stay, why she *must* fight. If there was no one else, she would have to be the person who stood between the good families, a good zone, and those who would destroy it.

She would never get Kaiden back. Or Davion.

But she had to fight for who was left—no matter how much it hurt.

She reached out and touched one of the basswood's heart-shaped leaves and exhaled.

At first, all she could do was stand there amid all the paraphernalia of loss and breathe. Then she leaned all her weight into the gray tree, the way she would often lean all her weight against her husband's back at the end of a long day.

But there were no warm arms to embrace her now.

Yet this basswood and her husband shared a similar steadiness. They shared a rooted sureness to the earth under her feet. With her hot cheek against the wood, somehow, magically, she found the solace she needed.

Gathering herself, she ran her hand down the length of the tree and found the display affixed to the trunk. She knelt so that she was eye level with the screen and pressed the button.

Videos of her husband laughing and smiling flashed across the screen. One showed the moment when he bent to scoop up their son, six at the time, and twirled him once before hooking him onto his hip.

Her mother would've selected these memories while Grace lay in the hospital. *I have to remember to thank her.*

Grace touched the screen, wishing she could feel warm flesh and blood under her fingertips. She wanted real breath on her face.

She sank to her knees and rested her head against the trunk of the tree.

"Davion," she whispered, tears blurring the grass beneath her. "I don't know if I can forgive you. I love you, but I don't know if I can forgive you. Not for this."

She touched the young sapling beside her. Kaiden's tree.

The breeze rustled the leaves, seeming to give her a response.

She sank deeper into the cold earth.

"But I will keep fighting for you—for both of you."

And with enough redemption stretching behind her, maybe she would find a way to forgive.

Enjoying Grace's story? It continues in book two *The City Within.*

Did you enjoy this book? You can make a BIG difference.

I don't have the same power as big New York publishers who can buy full-spread ads in magazines, and you won't see my covers on the side of a bus anytime soon, but what I *do* have are wonderful readers like you.

And honest reviews from readers garner more attention for my books and help my career more than anything else I could possibly do—and I can't get a review without you! So if you would be so kind, I'd be very grateful if you would post a review for this book.

It only takes a minute or so of your time, and yet you can't imagine how much it helps me. It can be as short as you like, and whether positive or negative, it really does help. I appreciate it so much and so do the readers looking for their next favorite read.

If you would be so kind, please find your preferred retailer at and leave a review for this book today.

Thank you so much!

Kory

GET YOUR FREE STORIES TODAY

Thank you so much for reading *The City Below*. I hope you're enjoying Grace's story. If you'd like more, I have a free, exclusive 2603 story for you. See Heron and Davion meet for the first time during one of his mother's scientific expeditions and learn how dangerous the outer zones are.

You can only read this story by signing up for my free newsletter. If you would like this story, you can get your copy by signing up for my free starter library at www.koryshrum.com

I will also send you free stories from the other series that I write.

Please add me to your address book so my emails aren't marked as spam. Once you sign up, check your email and make sure you received the story okay. Can't find it? Send me a message and I'll take care of it.

As to the newsletter itself, I send 1–2 newsletters a month with subscribers-only ebooks, writing updates, first looks, behind-the-scenes content—and, of course, photos of my very cute dog.

If this is not your cup of tea, you can follow me on social media in order to be notified of my new releases.

ACKNOWLEDGMENTS

Writing and releasing two books at once was a new challenge for me! Coupled with the fact that my mother died in July of this year means that I needed more support than usual. And to my surprise, I got it.

Special thanks to my first readers: Kimberly Benedicto, Kathrine Pendleton, Angela Roquet, and Monica La Porta. They gave me a good idea of what was and wasn't working as I crafted this new, exciting world.

Then came the professional help: Sarah Kolb-Williams did a great editorial job. Christian Bentulan's cover is awesome and Alexandra Amor, my wonderful assistant, helped with formatting (among many other things).

Last, but not least, my street team swept in the act as final cleanup crew. Shoutout to Larry Fletcher, Holly White, James Slater, Chris Christoforou, April Hardin, Phyllis Cazares, Dorkas, Chris De Francisci, Stan Hutchings, Melissa Izquierdo, Denise, Carmela Chateau, Valerie Ranne, Margaret Young, Rosemary Kenny, Mark Roberts, Murf, Fiona Agnew, Terry Monk, Rosemary Swierczewski, Kalynda Schock, Darryl, April, Debra Fortune, Victoria G. and Valarie Moss.

Thank you for reading the books and catching those final typos, as well as leaving reviews for the books. I appreciate your hard work so much.

ALSO BY KORY M. SHRUM

Dying for a Living series

Dying for a Living

Dying by the Hour

Dying for Her: A Companion Novel

Dying Light

Worth Dying For

Dying Breath

Dying Day

Shadows in the Water series

Shadows in the Water

Under the Bones

Danse Macabre

Carnival

Devil's Luck

What Comes Around

Overkill

Silver Bullet

Hell House

One Foot in the Grave

Blood Rain

First Light

Castle Cove series

Welcome to Castle Cove

Night Tide

The City 2603 series

The City Below

The City Within

The City Outside

Standalone Novels

Jack and the Fire Eater

A Magical Mending

Blade Born: A Borderlands Novel

Short Fiction

Thirst: new and collected stories

Final Cut: stories

Nonfiction

Who Killed My Mother? a memoir

A Well Cared for Human: self-love strategies for transforming
pain into power

Poetry (as K.B. Marie)

Birds & Other Dreamers

Questions for the Dead

You Can't Keep It

Learn more about Kory's work at www.koryshrum.com

ABOUT THE AUTHOR

USA TODAY bestselling author Kory M. Shrum has published more than thirty books, including the bestselling *Shadows in the Water* series.

She hosts two podcasts—*Who Killed My Mother?*, a true-crime podcast about her mother's tragic death, and *A Well Cared For Human*, focused on practical strategies for well-being and personal transformation.

She also publishes poetry under the name K.B. Marie.

When not writing, speaking, or pursuing one of her 300 hobbies, she can usually be found under thick blankets with snacks. The kettle is almost always on.

She lives in Michigan with her equally bookish wife, Kim, and their rescue dog, Max.

(Photo credit John K. Addis)

www.ingramcontent.com/pod-product-compliance
Lightning Source LLC
Chambersburg PA
CBHW071746190726
48292CB00003B/880